D0476458

Please return / renew by date shown.
You can renew it at:
norlink.norfolk.gov.uk
or by telephone: 0844 800 8006
Please have your library card & PIN ready

D S 9/19

The Pilgrims

Mary Shelley

ET REMOTISSIMA PROPE

Hesperus Classics

Hesperus Classics
Published by Hesperus Press Limited
4 Rickett Street, London SW6 1RU
www.hesperuspress.com

First published in *Keepsake*, 1829–37
This collection first published by Hesperus Press Limited, 2008

Foreword © Kamila Shamsie, 2008

Designed and typeset by Fraser Muggeridge studio
Printed in Jordan by Jordan National Press

ISBN: 978-1-84391-166-1

CONTENTS

FOREWORD

If you are near a fire, gather a group of listeners, and huddle round it with this book. Here are stories that are meant to be read, but also to be shared, filled as they are with storytellers and their audience. But be prepared for something in your life to change: storytelling, in each of these five tales, is not merely idle past-time, a way of filling empty hours. It is something more profound – a medium for revealing the most intimate details of character, the key component to affecting reconciliation, or a means of confirming deep loss.

And yet, perhaps such grandiose claims for the tales' transformative quality are merely the work of a mind still buried so deep within them that it has taken on their extravagance of spirit. (For I have started to write this only within minutes of finishing the stories, as if – allow me to claim this – one possessed.) Surely, you might say, for us twenty-first century readers there can be no connection between our listening ears, our reading eyes and the tales contained within the bindings of this book? Within each story, listeners and tellers are closely linked, yet in the world of fact we are entirely aware that however compelling each story is, it belongs to the world of fiction: its language and tone separating it by centuries from our contemporary lives. This does not impair our ability to appreciate the tightly constructed stories of love, mystery, suspense – but it is much too fanciful to suggest that our relationship with the storyteller should be anything other than that of listeners enjoying wondrous tales.

And yet, the further we plunge into these five stories, the more their overlapping echoes suggest some other – dare I say, über – story at work, trying to reveal certain truths in the guise of fiction. If we set aside the shortest of the tales – 'The False

Rhyme' – the other four stories share certain recurring motifs. Moreover, there is enough variation and excitement within each, that the motifs don't come across as lazy plotting or dull repetition, but as something more insistent.

The first of the motifs is that of the father as widower, raising a daughter he dearly loves. In 'The Pilgrims' and 'The Mourner', the widower-father is presented straightforwardly enough. In 'The Invisible Girl', though he is father to a son, it is his relationship to the girl he raises as his ward in which he seems more emotionally invested, and which is crucial to the story. And in 'The Dream' the story opens with the daughter mourning her father (the mother is not even mentioned, leaving us to surmise she died before her daughter was old enough to know her).

The second motif is that of the fraught triangle of father-daughter-lover. In 'The Pilgrims' the daughter's choice of husband causes her father to disown her. In 'The Invisible Girl' the father banishes his beloved ward from his house when he discovers who she has fallen in love with. And in both 'The Mourner' and 'The Dream' something about the circumstances of the father's death makes the daughter turn away from the man she loves.

The third of the motifs is that of a perilous sea. In 'The Mourner' there is death at sea; in 'The Invisible Girl' there are rumours of death at sea; in 'The Dream' a watery grave is narrowly averted. Only 'The Pilgrims' is without the threat or reality of drowning.

Even for those of us resistant to the notion of seeking a writer's biography in her works, these motifs make it almost impossible to stop from turning our gazes back to the one storyteller of all these tales: Mary Shelley. In her own lifetime, as now, the stories of her life were well-known: the mother dead when Mary was days old; the father who adored her; the married poet she eloped with, causing a terrible rift with her father; her husband's early death at sea. All these elements of Mary Shelley's life play themselves out in differing ways through the stories in this collection. And there is one other motif – most explicit in 'The False Rhyme', but evident in each story – the constancy of woman's love. Often this constancy is the very thing that causes her misery. She cannot stop loving either father or lover, not even when those two loves pull in opposite directions.

It is testimony to Shelley's skill as a teller of tales that the stories are never reduced to portraits of the author's psyche – anymore than *Frankenstein* is merely a portrait of anxiety about pregnancy or miscarriage, as some have suggested. But the adroitness with which Shelley uses stories within stories certainly gestures to the possibility that we should read her own story within those that she writes.

But ignore all this if you want. Forget everything you know about Mary Shelley and the circumstances of her personal life; there is still enough here to terrify and entertain. What might be failings elsewhere, here become strengths; so that when tales shared among strangers serve to unveil a bond between them, it doesn't feel like unbelievable coincidence, but an expression of fate. We are in the world of story, after all, with its own immutable logic that can only be undermined by the storyteller's hesitation – a hesitation entirely absent from Mary Shelley's work.

And so, 'The Pilgrims' delights with its interweaving structure, one story giving way to another just when you expect you're coming to a conclusion. 'The Invisible Girl' has a wonderful eeriness. 'The Mourner' is a deeply moving story, revealing the Gothic as a fine vehicle for tales of individuals suffering from profound depression, and the impact it has on those around them. 'The False Rhyme' is a masterclass in concision; and 'The Dream' has such a haunting quality to it that its presence lingers long after the tale has come to an end. I can feel its effect even now…

– Kamila Shamsie, 2008

The Pilgrims

THE PILGRIMS

The twilight of one of those burning days of summer whose unclouded sky seems to speak to man of happier realms, had already flung its broad shadows over the valley of Unspunnen; whilst the departing rays of a gorgeous sunset continued to glitter on the summits of the surrounding hills. Gradually, however, the glowing tints deepened, then grew darker and darker, until they finally yielded to the still more sober hues of night.

Beneath an avenue of lime trees, which, from their size and luxuriance, appeared almost coeval with the soil in which they grew, Burkhardt of Unspunnen wandered to and fro with uneasy step, as if some recent sorrow occupied his troubled mind. At times, he stood with his eyes steadfastly fixed on the earth, as if he expected to see the object of his contemplation start forth from its bosom; at other times, he would raise his eyes to the summits of the trees, whose branches, now gently agitated by the night breeze, seemed to breathe sighs of compassion in remembrance of those happy hours which had once been passed beneath their welcome shade. When, however, advancing from beneath them, he beheld the deep blue heavens with the bright host of stars, hope sprang up within him at the thoughts of that glory to which those heavens and those stars, lovely and beauteous as they seem, are but the faint heralds; and for a time dissipated the grief which had so long weighed heavily upon his heart.

From these reflections, which, from the intensity of his feelings, shut him out, as it were, from the busy world and its many paths, he was suddenly aroused by the tones of a manly voice addressing him.

Burkhardt advancing, beheld, standing in the light of the moon, two Pilgrims, clothed in the usual coarse and sombre garb, with their broad hats drawn over their brows.

'Praise be to God!' said the Pilgrim who had just before awakened Burkhardt's attention, and who, from his height and manner, appeared to be the elder of the two. His words were echoed by a voice whose gentle and faltering accents showed the speaker to be still but of tender years.

'Whither are you going, friends? What seek you here, at this late hour?' said Burkhardt. 'If you wish to rest you after your journey, enter and, with God's blessing, and my hearty welcome, recruit yourselves.'

'Noble sir, you have more than anticipated our petition,' replied the elder Pilgrim. 'Our duty has led us far from our native land, being bound on a pilgrimage to fulfil the vow of a beloved parent. We have been forced during the heat of the day to climb the steep mountain paths; and the strength of my brother, whose youth but ill befits him for such fatigues, began to fail, when the sight of your castle's towers, which the moon's clear beams discovered to us, revived our hopes. We resolved to beg a night's lodging under your hospitable roof, that we might be enabled, on tomorrow's dawn, to pursue our weary way.'

'Follow me, my friends,' said Burkhardt, as he, with quickened step, preceded them, that he might give some orders for their entertainment. The Pilgrims, rejoicing in so kind a reception, followed the knight in silence into a high-vaulted saloon, over which the tapers, that were placed in branches against the walls, cast a solemn but pleasing light, well in accordance with the present feelings of the parties.

The knight then discerned two countenances of great beauty, the pleasing impression of which was considerably heightened by the modest yet easy manner with which the youthful pair received their host's kind attentions. Much struck with their appearance and demeanour, Burkhardt was involuntarily led back into the train of thoughts from which their approach had aroused him; and the scenes of former days flitted before him as he recollected that, in this hall, his beloved child was ever wont to greet him with her welcome smile on his return from the battle or the chase – brief scenes of happiness, which had been followed by events that had cankered his heart, and rendered memory but an instrument of bitterness and chastisement.

Supper was soon after served, and the Pilgrims were supplied with the greatest attention, yet conversation wholly languished, for his melancholy reflections occupied Burkhardt, and respect, or perhaps a more kindly feeling, towards their host and benefactor, seemed to have sealed the lips of his youthful guests. After supper, however, a flask of the baron's old wine cheered his flagging spirits, and emboldened the elder Pilgrim to break through the spell which had chained them.

'Pardon me, noble sir,' said he, 'for I feel that it must seem intrusive in me to presume to seek the cause of that sorrow which thus severely oppresses you, and renders you so sad a spectator of the bounty and happiness which you liberally bestow upon others. Believe me, it is not the impulse of a mere idle curiosity that makes me express my wonder that you can thus dwell alone in this spacious and noble mansion, the prey to so deeply rooted a sorrow. Would that it were in our power, even in the slightest degree, to alleviate the cares of one who with such bounteous hand relieves the wants of his poorer brethren!'

'I thank you for your sympathy, good Pilgrim,' said the old noble, 'but what can it avail you to know the story of those griefs which have made this earth a desert, and which are, with rapid pace, conducting me where alone I can expect to find rest? Spare me, then, the pain of recalling scenes which I would fain bury in oblivion. As yet, you are in the spring of life, when no sad remembrance gives a discordant echo of past follies, or of joys irrecoverably lost. Seek not to darken the sunshine of your, I trust, unsullied youth, with a knowledge of those fierce, guilty beings who, in listening to the fiend-like suggestions of their passions, are led astray from the paths of rectitude, and tear asunder ties which nature, by the holiest bonds, had seemed to unite to their very souls.'

Burkhardt thus sought to avoid the entreaty of the Pilgrim. But the request was still urged with such earnest though delicate persuasion, and the rich tones of the stranger's voice awoke within him so many thoughts of days long, long past, that the knight felt himself almost irresistibly impelled to unburden his long-closed heart to one who seemed to enter into its feelings with a sincere cordiality.

'Your artless sympathy has won my confidence, my young friends,' said he, 'and you shall learn the cause of that sorrow which gnaws my heart.

'You see me now, indeed, here, lonely and forsaken, like a tree shaken by the tempest's violence. But fortune once looked upon me with her blandest smiles; and I felt myself rich in the consciousness of my prosperity, and the gifts which bounteous Heaven had bestowed. My powerful vassals made me a terror to those enemies which the protection, that I as ever ready to afford to the oppressed and helpless, brought against me. My rich and fertile possessions not only supplied my family with profusion, but enabled me, with liberal hand, to relieve the wants of the poor; and to exercise

6

the rights of hospitality in a manner justly becoming my state and my name. But of all the gifts which Heaven had showered upon me, that which I most prized was a wife, whose virtues had made her the idol of both the rich and the poor. But she who was already an angel, and unfitted for this grosser world, was too soon, alas, claimed by her kindred spirits. One brief year alone had beheld our happiness.

'My grief and anguish were most bitter, and would soon have laid me in the same grave with her, but that she had left me a daughter, for whose dear sake I struggled earnestly against my affliction. In her were now entered all my cares, all my hopes, all my happiness. As she grew in years, so did her likeness to her sainted mother increase, and every look and gesture reminded me of my Agnes. With her mother's beauty I had, with fond presumption, dared to cherish the hope that Ida would inherit her mother's virtues.

'Greatly did I feel the sad void that my irreparable loss had occasioned me, but the very thought of marrying again would have seemed to me a profanation to the memory of my Agnes. If, however, even for a single instant, I had entertained this disposition, one look at her child would have crushed it, and made me cling with still fonder hope to her, in the fond confidence that she would reward me for every sacrifice that I could make. Alas, my friends, this hope was built on an unsure foundation, and my heart is even now tortured when I think on those delusive dreams.

'Ida, with the fondest caresses, would dispel each care from my brow; in sickness and in health she watched me with the tenderest solicitude; her whole endeavour seemed to be to anticipate my wishes. But, alas, like the serpent, which only fascinates to destroy, she lavished these caresses and attentions to blind me, and wrap me in a fatal security.

7

'Many and deep were the affronts, revenged indeed, but not forgotten, which had long since caused (with shame, I avow it) a deadly hatred between myself and Rupert, Lord of Wädischwyl, which the slightest occasion seemed to increase to a degree of madness. As he dared no longer throw down the gauntlet, I having always in single combat come off the victor, he found means, much harder than steel or iron, to glut his revenge upon me.

'Duke Berchtold of Zähringen, one of those wealthy and powerful tyrants who are the very pests of that society of whose rights they ought to be the ready guardians, had made a sudden irruption on the peaceful inhabitants of the mountains, seizing their herds and flocks, and insulting their wives and daughters. Though possessed of great courage, yet being not much used to warfare, these unhappy men found it impossible to resist the tyrant, and hastened to entreat my instant succour. Without a moment's delay, I assembled my brave vassals, and marched against the spoiler. After a long and severe struggle, God blessed our cause, and our victory was complete.

'On the morning, that I was about to depart on my return to my castle, one of my followers announced to me that the duke had arrived in my camp, and wished an immediate interview with me. I instantly went forth to meet him, and Berchtold, hastening towards me with a smile, offered me his hand in token of reconciliation. I frankly accepted it, not suspecting that falsehood could lurk beneath so open and friendly an aspect.

'"My friend," said he, "for such I must call you, your valour in this contest having won my esteem, although I could at once convince you that I have just cause of quarrel with the insolent mountaineers. But, in spite of your victory in this unjust strife, into which doubtless you were induced to enter by the misrepresentations of those villains, yet as my nature abhors to prolong dissensions, I would willingly cease to think that we are enemies, and commence a friendship which, on my part, at least, shall not be broken. In token, therefore, that you do not mistrust a fellow soldier, return with me to my castle, that we may there drown all remembrance of our past disunion."

'During a long time, I resisted his importunity, for I had now been more than a year absent from my home; and was doubly impatient to return, as I fondly imagined that my delay would occasion much anxiety to my daughter. But the duke, with such apparent kindness and in such a courteous manner, renewed and urged his solicitations, that I could resist no longer.

'His highness entertained me with the greatest hospitality and unremitted attention. But I soon perceived that an *honest* man is more in his element amidst the toils of the battle than amongst the blandishments of a court, where the lip and the gesture carry welcome, but where the heart, to which the tongue is never the herald, is corroded by the unceasing strifes of jealousy and envy. I soon too saw that my rough and undisguised manners were an occasion of much mirth to the perfumed and essenced nothings who crowded the halls of the duke. I, however, stifled my resentment, when I considered that these creatures lived but in his favour; like those swarms of insects which are warmed into existence from the dunghill, by the sun's rays.

'I had remained the unwilling guest of the duke during some days, when the arrival of a stranger of distinction was announced with much ceremony. This stranger I found to be my bitterest foe, Rupert of Wädischwyl. The duke received him with the most marked politeness and attention; and more than once I fancied that I perceived the precedence of me was studiously given to my enemy. My frank yet haughty nature could ill brook this system of disparagement; and, besides, it seemed to me that I should but play the hypocrite if I partook of the same cup with the man for whom I entertained a deadly hatred.

'I resolved therefore to depart, and sought his highness to bid him farewell. He appeared much distressed at my resolution, and earnestly pressed me to avow the cause of my abrupt departure. I candidly confessed that the undue favour which I thought he showed to my rival was the cause.

'"I am hurt, deeply hurt," said the duke, affecting an air of great sorrow, "that my friend, and that friend the valiant Unspunnen, should think thus unjustly, dare I add, thus meanly of me. No, I have not even in thought wronged you; and to prove my sincerity and my regard for your welfare, know that it was not chance which conducted your adversary to my court. He comes in consequence of my eager wish to reconcile two men whom I so much esteem, and whose worth and excellence place them amongst the brightest ornaments of our favoured land. Let me, therefore," said he, taking my hand and the hand of Rupert, who had entered during our discourse, "let me have the enviable satisfaction of reconciling two such men, and of terminating your ancient discord. You cannot refuse a request so congenial to that holy faith which we all profess. Suffer me, therefore, to be the minister of peace; and to suggest that, in token and in confirmation of an act which will draw down Heaven's blessing on us all, you will permit our holy church to unite in one, your far-famed lovely daughter, with Lord Rupert's only son, whose virtues, if reports speak truly, render him no undeserving object of her love."

'A rage, which seemed in an instant to turn my blood into fire, and which almost choked my utterance, took possession of me.

'"What!" exclaimed I. "What, think you that I would thus sacrifice, thus cast away my precious jewel! Thus debase my beloved Ida? No, by her sainted mother, I swear that rather than see her married to his son, I would devote her to the cloister! Nay, I would rather see her dead at my feet, than suffer her purity to be sullied by such contamination!"

'"But for the presence of his highness," cried Rupert wrathfully, "your life should instantly answer for this insult! Nathless, I will well mark you, and watch you, too, my lord; and if you escape my revenge, you are more than man."

'"Indeed, indeed, my Lord of Unspunnen," said the duke, "you are much too rash. Your passion has clouded your reason; and, believe me, you will live to repent having so scornfully refused my friendly proposal."

'"You may judge me rash, my Lord Duke, and perhaps think me somewhat too bold, because I dare assert the truth, in the courts of princes. But since my tongue cannot frame itself to speak that which my heart does not dictate, and my plain but honest manner seems to displease you, I will, with your Highness' permission, withdraw to my own domain, whence I have been but too long absent."

'"Undoubtedly, my lord, you have my permission," said the duke haughtily, and at the same time turning coldly from me.

'My horse was brought, I mounted him with as much composure as I could command, and I breathed more freely as I left the castle far behind.

'During the second day's journey I arrived within a near view of my own native mountains; and I felt doubly invigorated, as their pure breezes were wafted towards me. Still the fond anxiety of a father for his beloved child, and that child his only treasure, made the way seem doubly long. But as I approached the turn of the road which is immediately in front of my castle, I almost then wished the way lengthened, for my joy, my hopes and my apprehensions crowded upon me almost to suffocation. "A few short minutes, however," I thought, "and then the truth, ill or good, will be known to me."

'When I came in full sight of my dwelling, all seemed in peace; nought exhibited any change since I had left it. I spurred my horse on to the gate; but as I advanced, the utter stillness and desertion of all around surprised me. Not a domestic, not a peasant was to be seen in the courts; it appeared as if the inhabitants of the castle were still asleep.

'"Merciful Heaven!" I thought. "What can this stillness forbode! Is she, is my beloved child dead?"

'I could not summon courage to pull the bell. Thrice I attempted, yet thrice the dread of learning the awful truth prevented me. One moment, one word, even one sign, and I might be a forlorn, childless, wretched man, for ever! None but a father can feel or fully sympathise in the agony of those moments! None but a father can ever fitly describe them! My existence seemed even to depend upon the breath of the first passer-by; and my eye shrank from observation lest it should encounter me.

'I was aroused from this inactive state by my faithful dog springing towards me to welcome my return with his boisterous caresses, and deep and loud toned expressions of his joy. Then the old porter, attracted by the noise, came to the gate, which he instantly opened; but, as he was hurrying forward to meet me, I readily perceived that some sudden and painful recollection checked his eagerness. I leaped from my horse quickly, and entered the hall. All the other domestics now came forward, except my faithful steward Wilfred, he who had been always the foremost to greet his master.

'"Where is my daughter? Where is your mistress?" I eagerly exclaimed. "Let me know but that she lives. Yet stop, stop; one moment, one short moment, ere you tell me I am lost for ever!"

'The faithful Wilfred, who had now entered the hall, threw himself at my feet, and with the tears rolling down his furrowed cheeks, earnestly pressed my hand, and hesitatingly informed me that my daughter *lived*; was well, he believed, but – had quitted the castle.

'"Now, speak more quickly, old man," said I hastily, and passionately interrupting him. "What is it you can mean? My daughter lives; my Ida is well, but she is *not here*. Now, have you and my vassals proved recreants, and suffered my castle in my absence to be robbed of its greatest treasure? Speak! Speak plainly, I command ye!"

'"It is with anguish, as great almost as your own can be, my beloved master, that I make known to you the sad truth, that your daughter has quitted her father's roof to become the wife of Conrad, the son of the Lord of Wädischwyl."

'"The wife of Lord Rupert's son! My Ida the wife of the son of him whose very name my soul loathes!"

'My wrath now knew no bounds; the torments of hell seemed to have changed the current of my blood. In the madness of my passion I even cursed my own dear daughter! Yes, Pilgrim, I even cursed her on whom I had so fondly doted; for whose sake alone life for me had any charms. Oh, how often since have I attempted to recall that curse! And these bitter tears, which even now I cannot control, witness how severe has been my repentance of that awful and unnatural act!

'Dreadful were the imprecations which I heaped upon my enemy, and deep was the revenge I swore. I know not to what fearful length my unbridled passion would have hurried me, had I not, from its very excess, sunk senseless into the arms of my domestics. When I recovered, I found myself in my own chamber, and Wilfred seated near me. Some time, however, elapsed before I came to a clear recollection of the past events; and when I did, it seemed as if an age of crime and misery had weighed me down and chained my tongue. My eye involuntarily wandered to that part of the chamber where hung my daughter's portrait. But this, the faithful old man – the who had not removed it, no doubt thinking that to do so would have offended me – had contrived to hide, by placing before it a piece of armour, which seemed as though it had accidentally fallen into that position.

'Many more days elapsed ere I was enabled to listen to the particulars of my daughter's flight; which I will, not to detain you longer with my griefs, now briefly relate. It appeared that, urged by the fame of her beauty, and by a curiosity most natural, I confess, to youth, Conrad of Wädischwyl had, for a long time, sought, but sought in vain, to see my Ida. Chance, at length, however, favoured him. On her way to hear mass at our neighbouring monastery, he beheld her; and beheld her but to love. Her holy errand did not prevent him from addressing her; and well the smooth-tongued villain knew how to gain the ear of one so innocent, so unsuspicious as my Ida! Too soon, alas, did his accursed flatteries win their way to her guiltless heart.

'My child's affection for her father was unbounded; and readily would she have sacrificed her life for mine. But when love has once taken possession of the female heart, too quickly drives he thence those sterner guests, reason and duty. Suffice it therefore to say she was won; and induced to unite herself to Wädischwyl, before my return, by his crafty and insidious argument that I should be more easily persuaded to give them my pardon and my blessing when I found that the step that she had taken was irrevocable. With almost equal art, he pleaded too that their union would doubtless heal the breach between the families of Wädischwyl and Unspunnen, and thus terminate that deadly hatred which my gentle Ida, ever the intercessor for peace, had always condemned. By this specious sophistry, my poor misguided child was prevailed upon to tear herself from the heart of a fond parent, to unite herself with an unprincipled deceiver, the son of that parent's most bitter enemy.'

The pain of these recollections so overcame Burkhardt, that some time elapsed ere he could master his feelings. At length he proceeded.

'My soul seemed now to have but one feeling, *revenge*. All other passions were annihilated by this master one; and I instantly prepared myself and my vassals to chastise this worse than robber. But such satisfaction was (I now thank God) denied me, for the Duke of Zähringen soon gave me memorable cause to recollect his parting words. Having attached himself with his numerous followers to my rival's party, these powerful chiefs suddenly invaded my domain. A severe struggle against most unequal numbers ensued. But, at length, though my brave retainers would fain have prolonged the hopeless strife, resolved to stop a needless waste of blood, I left the field to my foes; and, with the remnant of my faithful soldiers, hastened, in deep mortification, to bury myself within these walls. This galling repulse prevented all possibility of reconciliation with my daughter, whom I now regarded as the cause of my disgrace; and consequently, I forbad her name even to be mentioned in my presence.

'Years rolled on, and I had no intelligence of her until I learned by a mere chance that she had with her husband quitted her native land. Altogether, more than twenty, to me long, long years, have now passed since her flight; and though, when time brought repentance, and my anger and revenge yielded to better feelings, I made every effort to gain tidings of my poor child, I have not yet been able to discover any further traces of her. The chance of so doing was indeed rendered more difficult by the death of my faithful Wilfred, shortly after my defeat, and by the character of his successor, an individual of strict integrity, but of an austere temper and forbidding manners. Here, therefore, have I lived, a widowed, childless, heart-broken old man. But I have at least learned to bow to the dispensations of an All-Wise Providence, which has in its justice stricken me, for thus remorselessly cherishing that baneful passion which Holy Law so expressly forbids. Oh, how I have yearned to see my beloved child! How I have longed to clasp her to this withered, blighted heart! With scalding tears of the bitterest repentance have I revoked those deadly curses, which, in the plenitude of my unnatural wrath, I dared to utter daily. Ceaselessly do I now weary Heaven with my prayers to obliterate all memory of those fatal imprecations; or to let them fall on my own head, and shower down only its choicest blessings on that of my beloved child! But a fear, which freezes my veins with horror, constantly haunts me lest the maledictions which I dared to utter in my moments of demoniac vindictiveness, should, in punishment for my impiety, have been fulfilled.

'Often, in my dreams, do I behold my beloved child; but her looks are always in sadness, and she ever seems mildly but most sorrowfully to upbraid me, for having so inhumanly cast her from me. Yet she must, I fear, have died long ere now;

for, were she living, she would not, I think, have ceased to endeavour to regain the affections of a father who once loved her so tenderly. It is true that at first she made many efforts to obtain my forgiveness. Nay, I have subsequently learned that she even knelt at the threshold of my door, and piteously supplicated to be allowed to see me. But my commands had been so peremptory, and, as I before observed, the steward who had replaced Wilfred was of so stern and unbending a disposition, that, just and righteous as was this her last request, it was unfeelingly denied to her. Eternal Heaven! She whom I had loved as perhaps never father loved before – she whom I had fondly watched almost hourly lest the rude breeze of winter should chill her, or the summer's heat should scorch her – she whom I had cherished in sickness through many a livelong night, with a mother's devotion, and more than a mother's solicitude, even she, the only child of my beloved Agnes, and the anxious object of the last moments of her life, was spurned from my door! From this door whence no want goes unrelieved, and where the very beggar finds rest! And now, when I would bless the lips that even could say to me, "She lives," I can nowhere gather the slightest tidings of my child. Ah, had I listened to the voice of reason, had I not suffered my better feelings to be mastered by the wildest, and fellest passions, I might have seen her myself, and perhaps her children, happy around me, cheering the evening of my life. And when my last hour shall come, they would have closed my eyes in peace, and, in unfeigned sorrow have daily addressed to Heaven their innocent prayers for my soul's eternal rest; instead of the hirelings who will now execute the mummery of mourning, and impatiently hurry me to an unlamented, a lonely and an unhonoured grave. To those children also, would have descended that inheritance which must at my decease fall to an utter stranger, who bears not even my name.

'You now know, Pilgrims, the cause of my grief; and I see by the tears which you have so abundantly shed, that you truly pity the forlorn being before you. Remember him and his sorrows therefore ever in your prayers; and when you kneel at the shrine to which you are bound, let not those sorrows be forgotten.'

The elder Pilgrim in vain attempted to answer; the excess of his feelings overpowered his utterance. At length, throwing himself at the feet of Burkhardt, and casting off his Pilgrim's habits, he, with difficulty exclaimed,

'See here, thine Ida's son! And behold in my youthful companion, thine Ida's daughter! Yes, before you kneel the children of her whom you so much lament. We came to sue for that pardon, for that love, which we had feared would have been denied us. But, thanks be to God, who has mollified your heart, we have only to implore that you will suffer us to use our poor efforts to alleviate your sorrows; and render more bright and cheerful your declining years.'

In wild and agitated surprise, Burkhardt gazed intently upon them. It seemed to him as if a beautiful vision were before him, which he feared even a breath might dispel. When, however, he became assured that he was under the influence of no delusion, the tumult of his feelings overpowered him, and he sank senselessly on the neck of the elder Pilgrim, who, with his sister's assistance, quickly raised the old man, and by their united efforts restored him, ere long, to his senses. But when Burkhardt beheld the younger Pilgrim, the very image of his lost Ida, bending over him with the most anxious and tender solicitude, he thought that death had ended all his worldly sufferings, and that Heaven had already opened to his view.

'Great God!' at length he exclaimed. 'I am unworthy of these thy mercies! Grant me to receive them as I ought! I need not ask,' added he, after a pause, and pressing the Pilgrims to his bosom, 'for a confirmation of your statement, or of my own sensations of joy. All, all tells me that you are the children of my beloved Ida. Say, therefore, is your mother dead? Or dare I hope once more to clasp her to my heart?'

The elder Pilgrim, whose name was Hermann, then stated to him, that two years had passed since his parent had breathed her last in his arms. Her latest prayer was that Heaven would forgive her the sorrow she had caused her father, and forbear to visit her own error on her children's heads. He then added that his father had been dead many years.

'My mother,' continued Hermann, drawing from his bosom a small sealed packet, 'commanded me, on her deathbed, to deliver this into your own hands. "My son," she said, "when I am dead, if my father still lives, cast yourself at his feet, and desist not your supplications until you have obtained from him a promise that he will read this prayer. It will acquaint him with a repentance that may incite him to recall his curse; and thus cause the earth to lie lightly on all that will shortly remain of his once loved Ida. Paint to him the hours of anguish which even your tender years have witnessed. Weary him, my son, with your entreaties; cease them not until you have wrung from him his forgiveness."

'As you may suppose, I solemnly engaged to perform my mother's request; and as soon as our grief for the loss of so dear, so fond a parent, would permit us, my sister and myself resolved, in these pilgrim's habits, to visit your castle; and, by gradual means, to have attempted to win your affections, if we should have found you still relentless, and unwilling to listen to our mother's prayer.'

'Praise be to that God, my son,' said Burkhardt, 'at whose command the waters spring from the barren rock, that he has bidden the streams of love and repentance to flow once more from my once barren and flinty heart. But let me not delay to open this sad memorial of your mother's griefs. I wish you, my children, to listen to it, that you may hear both her exculpation and her wrongs.'

Burkhardt hid his face in his hands, and remained for some moments earnestly struggling with his feelings. At length, he broke the seal; and, with a voice which at times was almost overpowered, read aloud the contents.

My beloved father – if by that fond title your daughter may still address you, – feeling that my sad days are now numbered, I make this last effort, ere my strength shall fail me, to obtain at least your pity for her you once so much loved; and to beseech you to recall that curse which has weighed too heavily upon her heart. Indeed, my father, I am not quite that guilty wretch you think me. Do not imagine that, neglecting every tie of duty and gratitude, I could have left the tenderest of parents to his widowed lonely home, and have united myself with the son of his sworn foe, had I not fondly, most ardently, hoped, nay, had cherished the idea almost to certainty, that you would, when you found that I was a wife, have quickly pardoned a fault, which the fears of your refusal to our union had alone tempted me to commit. I firmly believed that my husband would then have shared with me my father's love, and have, with his child, the pleasing task of watching over his happiness and comfort. But never did I for an instant imagine that I was permanently wounding the heart of that father. My youth, and the ardour of my husband's persuasions, must plead some extenuation of my fault.

The day that I learned the news of your having pronounced against me that fatal curse, and your fixed determination never more to admit me to your presence, has been marked in characters indelible on my memory. At that moment, it appeared as if Heaven had abandoned me, had marked me for its reprobation as a parricide! My brain and my heart seemed on fire, whilst my blood froze in my veins. The chillness of death crept over every limb, and my tongue refused all utterance. I would have wept, but the source of my tears was dried within me.

How long I remained in this state I know not, as I at length became insensible, and remained so for some days. On returning to a full consciousness of my wretchedness, I would instantly have rushed to your abode, and cast myself at your feet, to wring from you, if possible, your forgiveness of my crime; but my limbs were incapable of all motion. Soon, too, I learned that the letters, which I dictated, were returned unopened; and my husband at last informed me that all his efforts to see you had been utterly fruitless.

Yet the moment I had gained sufficient strength, I went to the castle, but, unfortunately for me, even as I entered, I encountered a stern wretch, to whom my person was not unknown; and he instantly told me that my efforts to see his master would be useless. I used prayers and entreaties; I even knelt upon the bare ground to him. But so far from listening to me, he led me to the gate, and, in my presence, dismissed the old porter who had admitted me, and who afterwards followed my fortunes until the hour of his death. Finding that all my attempts were without hope, and that several of the old servants had been discarded on my account, with a heart completely broken, I succumbed to my fate, and abandoned all farther attempt.

After the birth of my son (to whose fidelity and love I trust this sad memorial) my husband, who, with the tenderest solicitude, employed every means in his power to divert my melancholy, having had a valuable property in Italy bequeathed to him, prevailed upon me to repair to that favoured and beauteous country. But neither the fond attentions of my beloved Conrad, nor the bright sunshine and luxurious breezes of that region of wonders, could overcome a grief so deeply rooted as mine; and I soon found that the gay garden of Europe had less charms for me, than my own dear native land, with its dark, pine-clad mountains.

Shortly after we had arrived at Rome, I gave birth to a daughter, an event which was only too soon followed by the death of my affectionate husband. The necessity of ceaseless attention to my infant, in some measure alleviated the intense anguish which I suffered from that most severe loss. Nevertheless, in the very depth of this sorrow, which almost overcharged my heart, Heaven only knows how often, and how remorsefully, while bending over my own dear children in sickness, have I called to mind the anxious fondness with which the tenderest and best of fathers used to watch over me!

I struggled long and painfully with my feelings, and often did I beseech God to spare my life, that I might be enabled to instruct my children in His holy love and fear, and teach them to atone for the error of their parent. My prayer has in mercy been heard; the boon I supplicated has been granted; and I trust, my beloved father, that if these children should be admitted to your affections, you will find that I have trained up two blessed intercessors for your forgiveness, when it shall have pleased Heaven to have called your daughter to her account before that dread tribunal where a sire's curse will plead so awfully against her. Recall then, oh beloved parent,

recall your dreadful malediction from your poor repentant
Ida! And send your blessing as an angel of mercy to plead
for her eternal rest. Farewell, my father, for ever! For ever,
farewell! By the cross, whose emblem her fevered lips now
press, by Him, who in his boundless mercy hung upon that
cross, your daughter, your once much loved Ida, implores you,
supplicates you, not to let her plead in vain!

'My child, my child!' sobbed Burkhardt, as the letter dropped from his hand. 'May the Father of All forgive me as freely as I from the depths of my wrung heart forgive you! Would that your remorseful father could have pressed you to his heart, with his own lips have assured you of his affection, and wiped away the tears of sorrow from your eyes! But he will cherish these beloved remembrances of you, and will more jealously guard them than his own life.'

Burkhardt passed the whole of the following day in his chamber, to which the good Father Jerome alone was admitted, as the events of the preceding day rendered a long repose absolutely necessary. The following morning, however, he entered the hall, where Hermann and Ida were impatiently waiting for him. His pale countenance still exhibited deep traces of the agitation he had experienced; but having kissed his children most affectionately, he smilingly flung round Ida's neck a massive gold chain, richly wrought, with a bunch of keys appended to it.

'We must duly install our Lady of the Castle,' said he, 'and invest her with her appropriate authorities. But, hark! From the sound of the porter's horn, it seems as if our hostess would have early calls upon her hospitality. Whom have we here?' continued he, looking out up the avenue. 'By St Hubert, a gay and gallant knight is approaching, who shall be right welcome

– that is, if my lady approve. Well, Willibald, what bring you? A letter from our good friend the abbot of St Anselm. What says he?'

I am sure that you will not refuse your welcome to a young knight, who is returning by your castle to his home, from the emperor's wars. He is well known to me, and I can vouch for his being a guest worthy of your hospitality, which will not be the less freely granted to him, because he does not bask in the golden smiles of fortune.

'No, no, that it shall not, my good friend; and if fortune frown upon him, he shall be doubly welcome. Conduct him hither, instantly, good Willibald.'

The steward hastened to usher in the stranger, who advanced into the hall, with a modest but manly air. He was apparently about twenty-five years of age; his person was such as might well, in the dreams of a young maiden, occupy no inconspicuous place.

'Sir Knight,' said Burkhardt, taking him cordially by the hand, 'you are right welcome to my castle, and such poor entertainment as it can afford. We must make you forget your wounds, and the rough usage of a soldier's life. But, soft, I already neglect my duty, in not first introducing our hostess,' added the aged knight, presenting Ida. 'By my faith,' he continued, 'judging from my lady's blushing smile, you seem not to have met for the first time. Am I right in my conjecture?'

'We *have* met, sir,' replied Ida, with such confusion as pleasantly implied that the meeting was not indifferently recollected, 'in the parlour of the Abbess of the Ursulines, at Munich, where I have sometimes been to visit a much valued friend.'

'The abbess,' said the young knight, 'was my cousin; and my good fortune more than once gave me the happiness of seeing in her convent this lady. But little did I expect that amongst these mountains the fickle goddess would again have so favoured a homeless wanderer.'

'Well, Sir Knight,' replied Burkhardt, 'we trust that fortune has been equally favourable to us. And now we will make bold to ask your name, and then, without useless and tedious ceremony, on the part of ourselves and our hostess, bid you again a hearty welcome.'

'My name,' said the stranger, 'is Walter de Blumfeldt. Though humble, it has never been disgraced, and with the blessing of Heaven, I hope to hand it down as honoured as I have received it.'

Weeks, months, rolled on, and Walter de Blumfeldt was still the guest of the Lord of Unspunnen; till, by his virtues, and the many excellent qualities which daily more and more developed themselves, he wound himself around Burkhardt's heart, which the chastened life of the old knight had rendered particularly susceptible of the kindlier feelings. Frequently would he now, with tears in his eyes, declare that he wished he could convince each and all with whom his former habits had caused any difference, how truly he forgave them, and desired their forgiveness.

'Would,' said he one day, in allusion to this subject, 'that I could have met my old enemy, the Duke of Zähringen, and with a truly heartfelt pleasure and joy have embraced him, and numbered him amongst my friends. But he is gathered to his fathers, and I know not whether he has left anyone to bear his honours.'

Each time that Walter had offered to depart, Burkhardt had found some excuse to detain him; for it seemed to him that in separating from his young guest, he should lose a link of that chain which good fortune had so lately woven for him. Hermann, too, loved Walter as a brother; and Ida fain would have imagined that she loved him as a sister: but her heart more plainly told her what her colder reasoning sought to hide. Unspunnen, who had for some time perceived the growing attachment between Walter and Ida, was not displeased at the discovery, as he had long ceased to covet riches; and had learned to prize the sterling worth of the young knight, who fully answered the high terms in which the Prior of St Anselm always spoke of him. Walking one evening under the shade of that very avenue where he had first encountered Hermann and Ida, he perceived the latter, at some little distance, in conversation with Walter. It was evident to Burkhardt that the young knight was not addressing himself to a very unwilling ear, as Ida was totally regardless of the loud cough with which Burkhardt chose to be seized at that moment; nor did she perceive him, until he exclaimed, or rather vociferated:

'Do you know, Walter, that, under this very avenue, two pilgrims, bound to some holy shrine, once accosted me; but that, in pity to my sins and forlorn condition, they exchanged their penitential journey for an act of greater charity, and have ever since remained to extend their kind cares to an aged and helpless relative but too little worthy of their love. One, however, of these affectionate beings is now about to quit my abode, and to pass through the rest of this life's pilgrimage with a helpmate in his toilsome journey, in the person of the fair daughter of the Baron de Leichtfeldt; and thus leave his poor companion to battle the storms of the world, with only the tedious society of an old man. Say, Sir Knight, will thy valour suffer that such wrong be done; or wilt *thou* undertake to conduct this forsaken pilgrim on her way, and guide her through the chequered paths of this variable life? I see by the lowliness with which you bend, and the colour which mantles in your cheek, that I speak not to one insensible to an old man's appeal. But soft, soft, Sir Knight, my Ida is not yet canonised, and therefore cannot afford to lose a hand, which inevitably must occur, if you continue to press it with such very ardent devotion. But what says our pilgrim, does she accept of thy conduct and service, Sir Knight?'

Ida, scarcely able to support herself, threw herself on Burkhardt's neck. We will not raise the veil which covers the awful moment that renders a man, as he supposes, happy or miserable for ever. Suffice it to say, that the day which made Hermann the husband of the daughter of the Baron de Leichtfeldt, saw Ida the wife of Walter de Blumfeldt.

Six months had passed rapidly away to the happy inhabitants of Unspunnen; and Burkhardt seemed almost to have grown young again; such wonders did the tranquillity which now reigned within him perform. He was therefore one of the most active and foremost in the preparations, which were necessary, in consequence of Walter suggesting that they should spend Ida's birthday in a favourite retreat of his and hers. This chosen spot was a beautiful meadow, in front of which meandered a small limpid river, or rather stream; at the back was a gorgeous amphitheatre of trees, the wide-spreading branches of which cast a refreshing shade over the richly enamelled grass.

In this beauteous retreat, were Burkhardt, Walter and his Ida, passing the sultry hours of noon, with all that flow of mirth which careless hearts can alone experience; when Walter, who had been relating some of his adventures at the Court of the

Emperor, and recounting the magnificence of the tournaments, turning to his bride, said:

'But what avails all that pomp, my Ida. How happy are we in this peaceful vale! We envy neither princes nor dukes their palaces, or their states. These woods, these glades, are worth all the stiffly trimmed gardens of the Emperor, and the great Monarch of France, to boot. What say you, my Ida, could you brook the ceremony of a court, and the pride of royalty? Methinks even the coronet of a duchess would but ill replace the wreath of blushing roses on your head.'

'Gently, my good husband,' replied Ida, laughing. 'They say, you know, that a woman loves these vanities too dearly in her heart, ever to despise them. Then how can you expect so frail a mortal as your poor wife to hold them in contempt? Indeed, I think,' added she, assuming an air of burlesque dignity, 'that I should make a lofty duchess, and wear my coronet with most becoming grace. And now, by my faith, Walter, I recollect that you have this day, like a true and gallant knight, promised to grant whatever boon I shall ask. On my bended knee, therefore, I humbly sue that if you know any spell or magic wile, to make a princess or a duchess for only a single day, that you will forthwith exercise your art upon me; just in order to enable me to ascertain with how much or how little dignity I could sustain such honours. It is no very difficult matter, Sir Knight: you have only to call in the aid of Number Nip, or some such handy workman of the woods. Answer, most chivalrous husband, for thy disconsolate wife rises not until her prayer is granted.'

'Why, Ida, you have indeed craved a rare boon,' replied Walter, 'and how to grant it may well puzzle my brain, till it becomes crazed with the effort. But, let me see, let me see,' continued he, musingly. 'I have it! Come hither, love, here is your throne,' said he, placing her on a gentle eminence richly covered with the fragrant wild thyme and the delicate harebell. 'Kings might now envy you the incense which is offered to you. And you, noble sir,' added he, addressing Burkhardt, 'must stand beside her Highness, in quality of chief counsellor. There are your attendants around you: behold that tall oak, he must be your Highness' poursuivant; and yonder slender mountain ashes, your trusty pages.'

'This is but a poor fulfilment of the task you have undertaken, Sir mummer,' said Ida, with a playful, and arch affectation of disappointment.

'Have patience for a brief while, fair dame,' replied Walter, laughing, 'for now must I awaken your Highness' men at arms.'

Then, taking from his side, a silver horn, he loudly sounded the melodious reveille. As he withdrew the instrument from his lips, a trumpet thrillingly answered to the call; and scarcely had its last notes died away, when, from the midst of the woods, as if the very trees were gifted with life, came forth a troop of horsemen, followed by a body of archers on foot. They had but just entirely emerged, when numerous peasants, both male and female, appeared in their gayest attire; and, together with the horsemen and the archers, rapidly and picturesquely ranged themselves in front of the astonished Ida, who had already abdicated her throne, and clung to the arm of Walter. They then suddenly divided; and twelve pages in richly emblazoned dresses advanced. After them followed six young girls, whose forms and features the Graces might have envied, bearing two coronets placed on embroidered cushions. In the rear of these, supporting his steps with his abbatial staff, walked the venerable Abbot of St Anselm, who, with his white beard flowing almost to his girdle, and his benign looks, that showed the pure commerce of the soul which gave life to an eye, the brightness of which seventy years had scarcely diminished, seemed to Ida a being of another world. The young girls then advancing, and kneeling before Walter and his wife, presented the coronets.

Ida, who had remained almost breathless with wonder, could now scarcely articulate, 'Dear, dear Walter, what is all this pomp – what does – what *can* it mean?'

'Mean! My beloved,' replied her husband, 'did you not bid me make you a duchess? I have but obeyed your high commands, and I now salute you, *Duchess* of Zähringen!"

The whole multitude then made the woods resound with the acclamation:

'*Long live the Duke, and Duchess of Zähringen!*'

Walter, having for some moments enjoyed the unutterable amazement of the now breathless Ida, and the less evident but perhaps equally intense surprise of Burkhardt, turning to the latter, said, 'My more than father, you see in me the son of your once implacable enemy, the Duke of Zähringen. He has been many years gathered to his fathers; and I, as his only son, have succeeded to his title, and his large possessions. My heart, my liberty, were entirely lost in the parlour of the Abbess of the Ursulines. But when I learned whose child my Ida was, and your sad story, I resolved ere I would make her mine, to win not only her love, but also your favour and esteem. How well I have succeeded, this little magic circle on my Ida's finger is my witness. It will add no small measure to your happiness, to know that my father had for many years repented of the wrongs which he had done you; and, as much as possible to atone for them, entrusted the education of his son to the care of this my best of friends, the Abbot of St Anselm, that he might learn to shun the errors into which his sire had unhappily fallen. And now,' continued he, advancing, and leading

Ida towards the Abbot, 'I have only to beg your blessing, and that this lady, whom through Heaven's goodness I glory to call my wife, be invested with those insignia of the rank which she is so fit to adorn.'

Walter, or as we must now call him, the Duke of Zähringen, with Ida, then lowly knelt before the venerable Abbot, whilst the holy man, with tears in his eyes, invoked upon them the blessings of Heaven. His Highness, then rising, took one of the coronets and, placing it on Ida's head, said, 'Mayst thou be as happy under this glittering coronet, as thou wert under the russet hood, in which I first beheld thee.'

'God and our Lady aid me!' replied the agitated Ida. 'And may He grant that I may wear it with as much humility. Yet thorns, they say, spring up beneath a crown.'

'True, my beloved,' said the duke, 'and they also grow beneath the peasant's homely cap. But the rich alchemy of my Ida's virtues will ever convert all thorns into the brightest jewels of her diadem.'

THE DREAM

The time of the occurrence of the little legend about to be narrated, was that of the commencement of the reign of Henry IV of France, whose accession and conversion, while they brought peace to the kingdom whose throne he ascended, were inadequate to heal the deep wounds mutually inflicted by the inimical parties. Private feuds, and the memory of mortal injuries, existed between those now apparently united; and often did the hands that had clasped each other in seeming friendly greeting, involuntarily, as the grasp was released, clasp the dagger's hilt, as fitter spokesman to their passions than the words of courtesy that had just fallen from their lips. Many of the fiercer Catholics retreated to their distant provinces; and while they concealed in solitude their rankling discontent, not less keenly did they long for the day when they might show it openly.

In a large and fortified chateau built on a rugged steep overlooking the Loire, not far from the town of Nantes, dwelt the last of her race, and the heiress of their fortunes, the young and beautiful Countess de Villeneuve. She had spent the preceding year in complete solitude in her secluded abode; and the mourning she wore for a father and two brothers, the victims of the civil wars, was a graceful and good reason why she did not appear at court, and mingle with its festivities. But the orphan countess inherited a high name and broad lands; and it was soon signified to her that the King, her guardian, desired that she should bestow them, together with her hand, upon some noble whose birth and accomplishments should entitle him to the gift. Constance, in reply, expressed her intention of taking vows, and retiring to a convent. The King earnestly and resolutely forbade this act, believing such an

33

idea to be the result of sensibility overwrought by sorrow, and relying on the hope that, after a time, the genial spirit of youth would break through this cloud.

A year passed, and still the countess persisted; and at last Henry, unwilling to exercise compulsion – desirous, too, of judging for himself of the motives that led one so beautiful, young, and gifted with fortune's favours, to desire to bury herself in a cloister – announced his intention, now that the period of her mourning was expired, of visiting her chateau; and if he brought not with him, the monarch said, inducement sufficient to change her design, he would yield his consent to its fulfilment.

Many a sad hour had Constance passed – many a day of tears, and many a night of restless misery. She had closed her gates against every visitant; and, like the Lady Olivia in *Twelfth Night*, vowed herself to loneliness and weeping. Mistress of herself, she easily silenced the entreaties and remonstrances of underlings, and nursed her grief as it had been the thing she loved. Yet it was too keen, too bitter, too burning, to be a favoured guest. In fact, Constance, young, ardent and vivacious, battled with it, struggled and longed to cast it off; but all that was joyful in itself, or fair in outward show, only served to renew it; and she could best support the burden of her sorrow with patience, when, yielding to it, it oppressed but did not torture her.

Constance had left the castle to wander in the neighbouring grounds. Lofty and extensive as were the apartments of her abode, she felt pent up within their walls, beneath their fretted roofs. The clear sky, the spreading uplands and the antique wood, associated to her with every dear recollection of her past life, enticed her to spend hours and days beneath their leafy coverts. The motion and change eternally working, as the wind stirred among the boughs, or the journeying sun rained its beams through them, soothed and called her out of that dull sorrow that clutched her heart with so unrelenting a pang beneath her castle roof.

There was one spot on the verge of the well-wooded park, one nook of ground, whence she could discern the country extended beyond, yet which was in itself thick set with tall umbrageous trees – a spot that she had forsworn, yet whither unconsciously her steps for ever tended, and where now again, for the twentieth time that day, she had unaware found herself. She sat upon a grassy mound, and looked wistfully on the flowers she had herself planted to adorn the verdurous recess – to her the temple of memory and love. She held the letter from the King that was the parent to her of so much despair. Dejection sat upon her features, and her gentle heart asked fate why, so young, unprotected and forsaken, she should have to struggle with this new form of wretchedness.

'I but ask,' she thought, 'to live in my father's halls – in the spot familiar to my infancy – to water with my frequent tears the graves of those I loved; and here in these woods, where such a mad dream of happiness was mine, to celebrate for ever the obsequies of Hope!'

A rustling among the boughs now met her ear – her heart beat quick – all again was still.

'Foolish girl!' she half muttered. 'Dupe of thine own passionate fancy: because here we met; because seated here I have expected, and sounds like these have announced, his dear approach; so now every coney as it stirs, and every bird as it awakens silence, speaks of him. O Gaspar – mine once – never again will this beloved spot be made glad by thee – never more!'

Again the bushes were stirred, and footsteps were heard in the brake. She rose; her heart beat high; it must be that silly Manon, with her impertinent entreaties for her to return. But the steps were firmer and slower than would be those of her waiting-woman; and now emerging from the shade, she too plainly discerned the intruder. Her first impulse was to fly – but once again to see him, to hear his voice – once again before she placed eternal vows between them, to stand together, and find the wide chasm filled that absence had made, could not injure the dead, and would soften the fatal sorrow that made her cheek so pale.

And now he was before, her, the same beloved one with whom she had exchanged vows of constancy. He, like her, seemed sad; nor could she resist the imploring glance that entreated her for one moment to remain.

'I come, lady,' said the young knight, 'without a hope to bend your inflexible will. I come but once again to see you, and to bid you farewell before I depart for the Holy Land. I come to beseech you not to immure yourself in the dark cloister to avoid one as hateful as myself – one you will never see more. Whether I die or live in Palestine, France and I are parted for ever!'

'Palestine!' said Constance. 'That were fearful, were it true; but King Henry will never so lose his favourite cavalier. The throne you helped to build, you still will guard. Nay, as I ever had power over thought of thine, go not to Palestine.'

'One word of yours could detain me – one smile – Constance – ' and the youthful lover knelt before her; but her harsher purpose was recalled by the image once so dear and familiar, now so strange and so forbidden.

'Linger no longer here!' she cried. 'No smile, no word of mine will ever again be yours. Why are you here – here, where the spirits of the dead wander, and claiming these shades as their own, curse the false girl who permits their murderer to disturb their sacred repose?'

'When love was young and you were kind,' replied the knight, 'you taught me to thread the intricacies of these woods; you welcomed me to this dear spot, where once you vowed to be my own – even beneath these ancient trees.'

'A wicked sin it was,' said Constance, 'to unbar my father's doors to the son of his enemy, and dearly is it punished!'

The young knight gained courage as she spoke; yet he dared not move, lest she, who, every instant, appeared ready to take flight, should be startled from her momentary tranquillity. But he slowly replied: 'Those were happy days, Constance, full of terror and deep joy, when evening brought me to your feet; and while hate and vengeance were as its atmosphere to yonder frowning castle, this leafy, starlit bower was the shrine of love.'

'*Happy?* Miserable days!' echoed Constance. 'When I imagined good could arise from failing in my duty, and that disobedience would be rewarded of God. Speak not of love, Gaspar! A sea of blood divides us for ever! Approach me not! The dead and the beloved stand even now between us: their pale shadows warn me of my fault, and menace me for listening to their murderer.'

'That am not I!' exclaimed the youth. 'Behold, Constance, we are each the last of our race. Death has dealt cruelly with us, and we are alone. It was not so when first we loved – when parent, kinsman, brother, nay, my own mother breathed curses on the house of Villeneuve; and in spite of all I blessed it. I saw thee, my lovely one, and blessed it. The God of peace planted love in our hearts, and with mystery and secrecy we met during many a summer night in the moonlit dells; and when daylight was abroad, in this sweet recess we fled to avoid its scrutiny, and here, even here, where now I kneel in supplication, we both knelt and made our vows. Shall they be broken?'

Constance wept as her lover recalled the images of happy hours. 'Never,' she exclaimed. 'O never! Thou knowest, or wilt soon know, Gaspar, the faith and resolves of one who dare not be yours. Was it for us to talk of love and happiness, when war, and hate, and blood were raging around! The fleeting flowers our young hands strewed were trampled by the deadly encounter of mortal foes. By your father's hand mine died; and little boots it to know whether, as my brother swore, and you deny, your hand did or did not deal the blow that destroyed him. You fought among those by whom he died. Say no more – no other word: it is impiety towards the unreposing dead to hear you. Go, Gaspar; forget me. Under the chivalrous and gallant Henry your career may be glorious; and some fair girl will listen, as once I did, to your vows, and be made happy by them. Farewell! May the Virgin bless you! In my cell and cloister-home I will not forget the best Christian lesson – to pray for our enemies. Gaspar, farewell!'

She glided hastily from the bower. With swift steps she threaded the glade and sought the castle. Once within the seclusion of her own apartment she gave way to the burst of grief that tore her gentle bosom like a tempest; for hers was that worst sorrow which taints past joys, making remorse wait upon the memory of bliss, and linking love and fancied guilt in such fearful society as that of the tyrant when he bound a living body to a corpse. Suddenly a thought darted into her mind. At first she rejected it as puerile and superstitious; but it would not be driven away. She called hastily for her attendant. 'Manon,' she said, 'didst thou ever sleep on St Catherine's couch?'

Manon crossed herself. 'Heaven forfend! None ever did, since I was born, but two: one fell into the Loire and was drowned; the other only looked upon the narrow bed, and returned to her own home without a word. It is an awful place; and if the votary have not led a pious and good life, woe betide the hour when she rests her head on the holy stone!'

Constance crossed herself also. 'As for our lives, it is only through our Lord and the blessed saints that we can any of us hope for righteousness. I will sleep on that couch tomorrow night!'

'Dear, my lady! And the King arrives tomorrow.'

'The more need that I resolve. It cannot be that misery so intense should dwell in any heart, and no cure be found. I had hoped to be the bringer of peace to our houses; and is the good work to be for me a crown of thorns? Heaven shall direct me. I will rest tomorrow night on St Catherine's bed: and if, as I have heard, the saint deigns to direct her votaries in dreams, I will be guided by her; and, believing that I act according to the dictates of Heaven, I shall feel resigned even to the worst.'

The King was on his way to Nantes from Paris, and he slept on this night at a castle but a few miles distant. Before dawn a young cavalier was introduced into his chamber. The knight had a serious, nay, a sad aspect; and all beautiful as he was in feature and limb, looked wayworn and haggard. He stood silent in Henry's presence, who, alert and gay, turned his lively blue eyes upon his guest, saying gently, 'So thou foundest her obdurate, Gaspar?'

'I found her resolved on our mutual misery. Alas, my liege, it is not, credit me, the least of my grief, that Constance sacrifices her own happiness when she destroys mine.'

'And thou believest that she will say nay to the gaillard chevalier whom we ourselves present to her?'

'Oh, my liege, think not that thought! It cannot be. My heart deeply, most deeply, thanks you for your generous condescension. But she whom her lover's voice in solitude – whose entreaties, when memory and seclusion aided the spell – could not persuade, will resist even your majesty's commands. She is bent upon entering a cloister; and I, so please you, will now take my leave: I am henceforth a soldier of the cross, and will die in Palestine.'

'Gaspar,' said the monarch, 'I know woman better than thou. It is not by submission nor tearful plaints she is to be won. The death of her relatives naturally sits heavy at the young countess' heart; and nourishing in solitude her regret and her repentance, she fancies that Heaven itself forbids your union. Let the voice of the world reach her – the voice of earthly power and earthly kindness – the one commanding, the other pleading, and both finding response in her own heart – and by my say and the Holy Cross, she will be yours. Let our plan still hold. And now to horse: the morning wears, and the sun is risen.'

The King arrived at the bishop's palace, and proceeded forthwith to mass in the cathedral. A sumptuous dinner succeeded, and it was afternoon before the monarch proceeded through the town beside the Loire to where, a little above Nantes, the Chateau Villeneuve was situated. The young countess received him at the gate. Henry looked in vain for the cheek blanched by misery, the aspect of downcast despair that he had been taught to expect. Her cheek was flushed, her manner animated, her voice scarce tremulous. 'She loves him not,' thought Henry, 'or already her heart has consented.'

A collation was prepared for the monarch; and after some little hesitation, arising from the cheerfulness of her mien, he mentioned the name of Gaspar. Constance blushed instead of turning pale, and replied very quickly, 'Tomorrow, good my liege; I ask for a respite but until tomorrow. All will then be decided. Tomorrow I am vowed to God – or –'

She looked confused, and the King, at once surprised and pleased, said, 'Then you hate not young de Vaudemont; you forgive him for the inimical blood that warms his veins.'

'We are taught that we should forgive, that we should love our enemies,' the countess replied, with some trepidation.

'Now, by Saint Denis, that is a right welcome answer for the nonce,' said the King, laughing. 'What ho! My faithful serving man, Don Apollo in disguise, come forward, and thank your lady for her love.'

In such disguise as had concealed him from all, the cavalier had hung behind, and viewed with infinite surprise the demeanour and calm countenance of the lady. He could not hear her words: but was this even she whom he had seen trembling and weeping the evening before? This she whose very heart was torn by conflicting passion, who saw the pale ghosts of parent and kinsman stand between her and the lover whom more than her life she adored? It was a riddle hard to solve. The King's call was in unison with his impatience, and he sprang forward. He was at her feet; while she, still passion-driven, overwrought by the very calmness she had assumed, uttered one cry as she recognised him, and sank senseless on the floor.

All this was very unintelligible. Even when her attendants had brought her to life, another fit succeeded, and then passionate floods of tears; while the monarch, waiting in the hall, eyeing the half-eaten collation and, humming some romance in commemoration of woman's waywardness, knew not how to reply to Vaudemont's look of bitter disappointment and anxiety. At length the countess' chief attendant came with an apology. 'Her lady was ill, very ill. The next day she would throw herself at the King's feet, at once to solicit his excuse, and to disclose her purpose.'

'Tomorrow – again tomorrow! Does tomorrow bear some charm, maiden?' said the King. 'Can you read us the riddle, pretty one? What strange tale belongs to tomorrow, that all rests on its advent?'

Manon coloured, looked down, and hesitated. But Henry was no tyro in the art of enticing ladies' attendants to disclose their ladies' counsel. Manon was, besides, frightened by the countess' scheme, on which she was still obstinately bent, so she was the more readily induced to betray it. To sleep in St Catherine's bed, to rest on a narrow ledge overhanging the deep rapid Loire, and if, as was most probable, the luckless dreamer escaped from falling into it, to take the disturbed visions that such uneasy slumber might produce for the dictate of Heaven, was a madness of which even Henry himself could scarcely deem any woman capable. But could Constance, her whose beauty was so highly intellectual, and whom he had heard perpetually praised for her strength of mind and talents, could *she* be so strangely infatuated! And can passion play such freaks with us? Like death, levelling even the aristocracy of the soul, and bringing noble and peasant, the wise and foolish, under one thraldom? It was strange – yet she must have her way. That she hesitated in her decision was much; and it was to be hoped that St Catherine would play no ill-natured part. Should it be otherwise, a purpose to be swayed by a dream might be influenced by other waking thoughts. To the more material kind of danger some safeguard should be brought.

There is no feeling more awful than that which invades a weak human heart bent upon gratifying its ungovernable impulses in contradiction to the dictates of conscience.

42

Forbidden pleasures are said to be the most agreeable. It may be so to rude natures, to those who love to struggle, combat and contest; who find happiness in a fray, and joy in the conflict of passion. But softer and sweeter was the gentle spirit of Constance; and love and duty contending crushed and tortured her poor heart. To commit her conduct to the inspirations of religion, or, if it was so to be named, of superstition, was a blessed relief. The very perils that threatened her undertaking gave a zest to it; to dare for his sake was happiness; the very difficulty of the way that led to the completion of her wishes at once gratified her love and distracted her thoughts from her despair. Or if it was decreed that she must sacrifice all, the risk of danger and of death were of trifling import in comparison with the anguish that would then be her portion for ever.

The night threatened to be stormy, the raging wind shook the casements, and the trees waved their huge shadowy arms, as giants might in fantastic dance and mortal broil. Constance and Manon, unattended, quitted the chateau by a postern, and began to descend the hillside. The moon had not yet risen; and though the way was familiar to both, Manon tottered and trembled, while the countess, drawing her silken cloak around her, walked with a firm step down the steep. They came to the river's side, where a small boat was moored, and one man was in waiting. Constance stepped lightly in, and then aided her fearful companion. In a few moments they were in the middle of the stream. The warm, tempestuous, animating, equinoctial wind swept over them. For the first time since her mourning, a thrill of pleasure swelled the bosom of Constance. She hailed the emotion with double joy. 'It cannot be,' she thought, 'that Heaven will forbid me to love one so brave, so generous and so good as the noble Gaspar. Another I can never love. I shall die if divided from him; and this heart, these limbs, so alive with glowing sensation, are they already predestined to an early grave? Oh, no! Life speaks aloud within them. I shall live to love. Do not all things love – the winds as they whisper to the rushing waters, the waters as they kiss the flowery banks, and speed to mingle with the sea? Heaven and earth are sustained by, live through, love; and shall Constance alone, whose heart has ever been a deep, gushing, overflowing well of true affection, be compelled to set a stone upon the fount to lock it up for ever?'

These thoughts bade fair for pleasant dreams; and perhaps the countess, an adept in the blind god's lore, therefore indulged them the more readily. But as thus she was engrossed by soft emotions, Manon caught her arm. 'Lady, look,' she cried. 'It comes yet the oars have no sound. Now the Virgin shield us! Would we were at home!'

A dark boat glided by them. Four rowers, habited in black cloaks, pulled at oars that, as Manon said, gave no sound. Another sat at the helm. Like the rest, his person was veiled in a dark mantle, but he wore no cap; and though his face was turned from them, Constance recognised her lover. 'Gaspar,' she cried aloud, 'dost thou live?' But the figure in the boat neither turned its head nor replied, and quickly it was lost in the shadowy waters.

How changed now was the fair countess' reverie! Already Heaven had begun its spell, and unearthly forms were around, as she strained her eyes through the gloom. Now she saw and now she lost view of the bark that occasioned her terror; and now it seemed that another was there, which held the spirits of the dead; and her father waved to her from shore, and her brothers frowned on her.

Meanwhile they neared the landing. Her bark was moored in a little cove, and Constance stood upon the bank. Now she trembled, and half yielded to Manon's entreaty to return, till the unwise *suivante* mentioned the King's and de Vaudemont's name, and spoke of the answer to be given tomorrow. What answer, if she turned back from her intent?

She now hurried forward up the broken ground of the bank, and then along its edge, till they came to a hill which abruptly hung over the tide. A small chapel stood near. With trembling fingers the countess drew forth the key and unlocked its door. They entered. It was dark – save that a little lamp, flickering in the wind, showed an uncertain light from before the figure of St Catherine. The two women knelt; they prayed; and then, rising, with a cheerful accent the countess bade her attendant goodnight. She unlocked a little low iron door. It opened on a narrow cavern. The roar of waters was heard beyond. 'Thou mayest not follow, my poor Manon,' said Constance, 'nor dost thou much desire: this adventure is for me alone.'

It was hardly fair to leave the trembling servant in the chapel alone, who had neither hope nor fear, nor love nor grief to beguile her; but, in those days, esquires and waiting-women often played the part of subalterns in the army, gaining knocks and no fame. Besides, Manon was safe in holy ground. The countess meanwhile pursued her way, groping in the dark through the narrow tortuous passage. At length what seemed light to her long-darkened sense gleamed on her. She reached an open cavern in the overhanging hill's side, looking over the rushing tide beneath. She looked out upon the night. The waters of the Loire were speeding, as since that day have they ever sped – changeful, yet the same; the heavens were thickly veiled with clouds, and the wind in the trees was as mournful and ill-omened as if it rushed round a murderer's tomb. Constance shuddered a little, and looked upon her bed –

a narrow ledge of earth and a moss-grown stone bordering on the very verge of the precipice. She doffed her mantle – such was one of the conditions of the spell; she bowed her head, and loosened the tresses of her dark hair; she bared her feet; and thus, fully prepared for suffering to the utmost the chill influence of the cold night, she stretched herself on the narrow couch that scarce afforded room for her repose, and whence, if she moved in sleep, she must be precipitated into the cold waters below.

At first it seemed to her as if she never should sleep again. No great wonder that exposure to the blast and her perilous position should forbid her eyelids to close. At length she fell into a reverie so soft and soothing that she wished even to watch; and then by degrees her senses became confused; and now she was on St Catherine's bed – the Loire rushing beneath, and the wild wind sweeping by – and now – oh whither? – and what dreams did the saint send, to drive her to despair, or to bid her be blessed for ever?

Beneath the rugged hill, upon the dark tide, another watched, who feared a thousand things, and scarce dared hope. He had meant to precede the lady on her way, but when he found that he had outstayed his time, with muffled oars and breathless haste he had shot by the bark that contained his Constance, nor even turned at her voice, fearful to incur her blame, and her commands to return. He had seen her emerge from the passage, and shuddered as she leaned over the cliff. He saw her step forth, clad as she was in white, and could mark her as she lay on the edge beetling above. What a vigil did the lovers keep! She given up to visionary thoughts, he knowing – and the consciousness thrilled his bosom with strange emotion – that love, and love for him, had led her to that perilous couch; and that while dangers surrounded her in every shape, she was alive only to a small still voice that whispered to her heart the dream that was to decide their destinies. She slept perhaps – but he waked and watched; and night wore away, as now praying, now entranced by alternating hope and fear, he sat in his boat, his eyes fixed on the white garb of the slumberer above.

Morning – was it morning that struggled in the clouds? Would morning ever come to waken her? And had she slept? And what dreams of weal or woe had peopled her sleep? Gaspar grew impatient. He commanded his boatmen still to wait, and he sprang forward, intent on clambering the precipice. In vain they urged the danger, nay, the impossibility of the attempt; he clung to the rugged face of the hill, and found footing where it would seem no footing was. The acclivity, indeed, was not high; the dangers of St Catherine's bed arising from the likelihood that any one who slept on so narrow a couch would be precipitated into the waters beneath. Up the steep ascent Gaspar continued to toil, and at last reached the roots of a tree that grew near the summit. Aided by its branches, he made good his stand at the very extremity of the ledge, near the pillow on which lay the uncovered head of his beloved. Her hands were folded on her bosom; her dark hair fell round her throat and pillowed her cheek; her face was serene. Sleep was there in all its innocence and in all its helplessness; every wilder emotion was hushed, and her bosom heaved in regular breathing. He could see her heart beat as it lifted her fair hands crossed above. No statue hewn of marble in monumental effigy was ever half so fair; and within that surpassing form dwelled a soul true, tender, self-devoted and affectionate as ever warmed a human breast.

With what deep passion did Gaspar gaze, gathering hope from the placidity of her angel countenance! A smile wreathed her lips, and he too involuntarily smiled, as he hailed the happy omen; when suddenly her cheek was flushed, her bosom heaved, a tear stole from her dark lashes, and then a whole shower fell, as starting up she cried, 'No! He shall not die! I will unloose his chains! I will save him!' Gaspar's hand was there. He caught her light form ready to fall from the perilous couch. She opened her eyes and beheld her lover, who had watched over her dream of fate, and who had saved her.

Manon also had slept well, dreaming or not, and was startled in the morning to find that she waked surrounded by a crowd. The little desolate chapel was hung with tapestry, the altar adorned with golden chalices; the priest was chanting mass to a goodly array of kneeling knights. Manon saw that King Henry was there; and she looked for another whom she found not, when the iron door of the cavern passage opened, and Gaspar de Vaudemont entered from it, leading the fair form of Constance, who, in her white robes and dark dishevelled hair, with a face in which smiles and blushes contended with deeper emotion, approached the altar, and, kneeling with her lover, pronounced the vows that united them for ever.

It was long before the happy Gaspar could win from his lady the secret of her dream. In spite of the happiness she now enjoyed, she had suffered too much not to look back even with terror to those days when she thought love a crime, and every event connected with them wore an awful aspect. Many a vision, she said, she had that fearful night. She had seen the spirits of her father and brothers in Paradise; she had beheld Gaspar victoriously combating among the infidels; she had beheld him in King Henry's court, favoured and beloved; and she herself – now pining in a cloister, now a bride, now grateful to Heaven for the full measure of bliss presented to her, now weeping away her sad days – till suddenly she thought herself in Paynim land; and the saint herself, St Catherine, guiding her unseen through the city of the infidels. She entered a palace, and beheld the miscreants rejoicing in victory; and then, descending to the dungeons beneath, they groped their way through damp vaults, and low, mildewed passages, to one cell, darker and more frightful than the rest. On the floor lay one with soiled and tattered garments, with unkempt locks and wild, matted beard. His cheek was worn and thin; his eyes had lost their fire; his form was a mere skeleton; the chains hung loosely on the fleshless bones.

'And was it my appearance in that attractive state and winning costume that softened the hard heart of Constance?' asked Gaspar, smiling at this painting of what would never be.

'Even so,' replied Constance. 'For my heart whispered to me that this was my doing; and who could recall the life that waned in your pulses – who restore, save the destroyer? My heart never warmed to my living, happy knight as then it did to his wasted image as it lay, in the visions of night, at my feet. A veil fell from my eyes; a darkness was dispelled from before me. Methought I then knew for the first time what life and what death was. I was bid believe that to make the living happy was not to injure the dead; and I felt how wicked and how vain was that false philosophy that placed virtue and good in hatred and unkindness. You should not die; I would loosen your chains and save you, and bid you live for love. I sprang forward, and the death I deprecated for you would, in my presumption, have been mine – then, when first I felt the real value of life – but that your arm was there to save me, your dear voice to bid me be blessed for evermore.'

THE FALSE RHYME

Come, tell me where the maid is found
Whose heart can love without deceit,
And I will range the world around
To sigh one moment at her feet.
– Thomas Moore

On a fine July day, the fair Margaret, Queen of Navarre, then on a visit to her royal brother, had arranged a rural feast for the morning following, which Francis declined attending. He was melancholy; and the cause was said to be some lover's quarrel with a favourite dame. The morrow came, and dark rain and murky clouds destroyed at once the schemes of the courtly throng. Margaret was angry, and she grew weary: her only hope for amusement was in Francis, and he had shut himself up – an excellent reason why she should the more desire to see him. She entered his apartment. He was standing at the casement, against which the noisy shower beat, writing with a diamond on the glass. Two beautiful dogs were his sole companions. As Queen Margaret entered, he hastily let down the silken curtain before the window, and looked a little confused.

'What treason is this, my liege,' said the Queen, 'that crimsons your cheek? I must see the same.'

'It is treason,' replied the King, 'and therefore, sweet sister, thou mayest not see it.'

This the more excited Margaret's curiosity, and a playful contest ensued. Francis at last yielded: he threw himself on a huge high-backed settee; and as the lady drew back the curtain with an arch smile, he grew grave and sentimental, as he reflected on the cause that had inspired his libel against all womankind.

'What have we here?' cried Margaret. 'Nay, this is lese-majeste:

'*Souvent femme varie,*
Bien fou qui s'y fie!'

'Very little change would greatly amend your couplet. Would it not run better thus:

'*Souvent homme varie,*
Bien folle qui s'y fie?'

'I could tell you twenty stories of man's inconstancy.'

'I will be content with one true tale of woman's fidelity,' said Francis, drily, 'but do not provoke me. I would fain be at peace with the soft Mutabilities, for thy dear sake.'

'I defy your grace,' replied Margaret, rashly, 'to instance the falsehood of one noble and well-reputed dame.'

'Not even Emilie de Lagny?' asked the King.

This was a sore subject for the queen. Emilie had been brought up in her own household, the most beautiful and the most virtuous of her maids of honour. She had long loved the Sire de Lagny, and their nuptials were celebrated with rejoicings but little ominous of the result. De Lagny was accused but a year after of traitorously yielding to the emperor a fortress under his command, and he was condemned to perpetual imprisonment. For some time Emilie seemed inconsolable, often visiting the miserable dungeon of her husband, and suffering on her return, from witnessing his wretchedness, such paroxysms of grief as threatened her life. Suddenly, in the midst of her sorrow, she disappeared; and enquiry only divulged the disgraceful fact, that she had escaped from

France, bearing her jewels with her, and accompanied by her page, Robinet Leroux. It was whispered that, during their journey, the lady and the stripling often occupied one chamber; and Margaret, enraged at these discoveries, commanded that no further quest should be made for her lost favourite.

Taunted now by her brother, she defended Emilie, declaring that she believed her to be guiltless, even going so far as to boast that within a month she would bring proof of her innocence.

'Robinet was a pretty boy,' said Francis, laughing.

'Let us make a bet,' cried Margaret. 'If I lose, I will bear this vile rhyme of thine as a motto to my shame to my grave; if I win –'

'I will break my window, and grant thee whatever boon thou askest.'

The result of this bet was long sung by troubadour and minstrel. The Queen employed a hundred emissaries – published rewards for any intelligence of Emilie – all in vain. The month was expiring, and Margaret would have given many bright jewels to redeem her word. On the eve of the fatal day, the jailer of the prison in which the Sire de Lagny was confined sought an audience of the Queen; he brought her a message from the knight to say that if the Lady Margaret would ask his pardon as her boon, and obtain from her royal brother that he might be brought before him, her bet was won. Fair Margaret was very joyful, and readily made the desired promise. Francis was unwilling to see his false servant, but he was in high good humour, for a cavalier had that morning brought intelligence of a victory over the Imperialists. The messenger himself was lauded in the despatches as the most fearless and bravest knight in France. The King loaded him with presents, only regretting that a vow prevented the soldier from raising his visor or declaring his name.

That same evening as the setting sun shone on the lattice on which the ungallant rhyme was traced, Francis reposed on the same settee, and the beautiful Queen of Navarre, with triumph in her bright eyes, sat beside him. Attended by guards, the prisoner was brought in. His frame was attenuated by privation, and he walked with tottering steps. He knelt at the feet of Francis, and uncovered his head; a quantity of rich golden hair then escaping fell over the sunken cheeks and pallid brow of the suppliant. 'We have treason here!' cried the King. 'Sir jailer, where is your prisoner?'

'Sire, blame him not,' said the soft faltering voice of Emilie. 'Wiser men than he have been deceived by woman. My dear lord was guiltless of the crime for which he suffered. There was but one mode to save him: I assumed his chains – he escaped with poor Robinet Leroux in my attire. He joined your army: the young and gallant cavalier who delivered the despatches to your grace, whom you overwhelmed with honours and reward, is my own Enguerrard de Lagny. I waited but for his arrival with testimonials of his innocence, to declare myself to my lady, the Queen. Has she not won her bet? And the boon she asks –'

'Is de Lagny's pardon,' said Margaret, as she also knelt to the King. 'Spare your faithful vassal, sire, and reward this lady's truth.'

Francis first broke the false-speaking window, then he raised the ladies from their supplicatory posture.

In the tournament given to celebrate this 'Triumph of Ladies', the Sire de Lagny bore off every prize; and surely there was more loveliness in Emilie's faded cheek, more grace in her emaciated form – type as they were of truest affection – than in the prouder bearing and fresher complexion of the most brilliant beauty in attendance on the courtly festival.

THE INVISIBLE GIRL

This slender narrative has no pretensions to the regularity of a story, or the development of situations and feelings; it is but a slight sketch, delivered nearly as it was narrated to me by one of the humblest of the actors concerned. Nor will I spin out a circumstance interesting principally from its singularity and truth, but narrate, as concisely as I can, how I was surprised on visiting what seemed a ruined tower, crowning a bleak promontory overhanging the sea that flows between Wales and Ireland, to find that though the exterior preserved all the savage rudeness that betokened many a war with the elements, the interior was fitted up somewhat in the guise of a summer-house, for it was too small to deserve any other name. It consisted but of the ground floor, which served as an entrance, and one room above, which was reached by a staircase made out of the thickness of the wall. This chamber was floored and carpeted, decorated with elegant furniture; and, above all, to attract the attention and excite curiosity, there hung over the chimney piece – for to preserve the apartment from damp a fireplace had been built evidently since it had assumed a guise so dissimilar to the object of its construction – a picture simply painted in watercolours, which seemed more than any part of the adornments of the room to be at war with the rudeness of the building, the solitude in which it was placed, and the desolation of the surrounding scenery. This drawing represented a lovely girl in the very pride and bloom of youth; her dress was simple, in the fashion of the day (remember, reader, I write at the beginning of the eighteenth century), her countenance was embellished by a look of mingled innocence and intelligence, to which was added the imprint of serenity of soul and natural cheerfulness. She was reading one of those folio romances which have so long been the delight of the enthusiastic and young; her mandolin was at her feet; her parakeet perched on a huge mirror near her; the arrangement of furniture and hangings gave token of a luxurious dwelling, and her attire also evidently that of home and privacy, yet bore with it an appearance of ease and girlish ornament, as if she wished to please. Beneath this picture was inscribed in golden letters, 'The Invisible Girl'.

Rambling about a country nearly uninhabited, having lost my way, and being overtaken by a shower, I had lighted on this dreary-looking tenement, which seemed to rock in the blast, and to be hung up there as the very symbol of desolation. I was gazing wistfully and cursing inwardly my stars which led me to a ruin that could afford no shelter, though the storm began to pelt more seriously than before, when I saw an old woman's head popped out from a kind of loophole, and as suddenly withdrawn. A minute after, a feminine voice called to me from within, and penetrating a little brambly maze that screened a door, which I had not before observed, so skilfully had the planter succeeded in concealing art with nature, I found the good dame standing on the threshold and inviting me to take refuge within. 'I had just come up from our cot hard by,' she said, 'to look after the things, as I do every day, when the rain came on – will ye walk up till it is over?' I was about to observe that the cot hard by, at the venture of a few rain drops, was better than a ruined tower, and to ask my kind hostess whether 'the things' were pigeons or crows that she was come to look after, when the matting of the floor and the carpeting of the staircase struck my eye. I was still more surprised when I saw the room above; and beyond all, the picture and its singular inscription, naming her invisible, whom the painter had coloured forth into very agreeable visibility, awakened my most lively curiosity. The result of this, of my exceeding polite-ness towards the old woman, and her own natural garrulity, was a kind of garbled narrative which my imagination eked out, and future enquiries rectified, till it assumed the following form.

Some years before in the afternoon of a September day, which, though tolerably fair, gave many tokens of a tempestuous evening, a gentleman arrived at a little coast town about ten miles from this place. He expressed his desire to hire a boat to carry him to the town of about fifteen miles further on the coast. The menaces which the sky held forth made the fishermen loathe to venture, till at length two – one the father of a numerous family, bribed by the bountiful reward the stranger promised, the other, the son of my hostess, induced by youthful daring – agreed to undertake the voyage. The wind was fair, and they hoped to make good way before nightfall, and to get into port ere the rising of the storm. They pushed off with good cheer, at least the fishermen did; as for the stranger, the deep mourning which he wore was not half so black as the melan-choly that wrapped his mind. He looked as if he had never smiled – as if some unutterable thought, dark as night and bitter as death, had built its nest within his bosom, and brooded therein eternally. He did not mention his name, but one of the villagers recognised him as Henry Vernon, the son of a baronet who possessed a mansion about three miles distant from the town for which he was bound. This mansion was almost abandoned by the family; but Henry had, in a romantic fit, visited it about three years before, and Sir Peter had been down there during the previous spring for about a couple of months.

The boat did not make so much way as was expected; the breeze failed them as they got out to sea, and they were fain with oar as well as sail, to try to weather the promontory that jutted out between them and the spot they desired to reach.

They were yet far distant when the shifting wind began to exert its strength, and to blow with violent though unequal puffs. Night came on pitchy dark, and the howling waves rose and broke with frightful violence, menacing to overwhelm the tiny bark that dared resist their fury. They were forced to lower every sail, and take to their oars; one man was obliged to bale out the water, and Vernon himself took an oar, and, rowing with desperate energy, equalled the force of the more practised boatmen. There had been much talk between the sailors before the tempest came on; now, except a brief command, all were silent. One thought of his wife and children, and silently cursed the caprice of the stranger that endangered in its effects not only his life, but their welfare; the other feared less, for he was a daring lad, but he worked hard, and had no time for speech; while Vernon, bitterly regretting the thoughtlessness which had made him cause others to share a peril, unimportant as far as he himself was concerned, now tried to cheer them with a voice full of animation and courage, and now pulled yet more strongly at the oar he held. The only person who did not seem wholly intent on the work he was about, was the man who baled; every now and then he gazed intently round, as if the sea held afar off, on its tumultuous waste, some object that he strained his eyes to discern. But all was blank, except as the crests of the high waves showed themselves, or far out on the verge of the horizon, a kind of lifting of the clouds betokened greater violence for the blast. At length he exclaimed, 'Yes, I see it! The larboard oar! Now! If we can make yonder light, we are saved!' Both the rowers instinctively turned their heads – but cheerless darkness answered their gaze.

'You cannot see it,' cried their companion, 'but we are nearing it; and, please God, we shall outlive this night.' Soon he took the oar from Vernon's hand, who, quite exhausted, was failing in his strokes. He rose and looked for the beacon which promised them safety; it glimmered with so faint a ray, that now he said, 'I see it,' and again, 'It is nothing.' Still, as they made way, it dawned upon his sight, growing more steady and distinct as it beamed across the lurid waters, which themselves became smoother, so that safety seemed to arise from the bosom of the ocean under the influence of that flickering gleam.

'What beacon is it that helps us at our need?' asked Vernon, as the men, now able to manage their oars with greater ease, found breath to answer his question.

'A fairy one, I believe,' replied the elder sailor, 'yet no less a true: it burns in an old tumble-down tower, built on the top of a rock which looks over the sea. We never saw it before this summer; and now each night it is to be seen – at least when it is looked for, for we cannot see it from our village – and it is such an out of the way place that no one has need to go near it, except through a chance like this. Some say it is burned by witches, some say by smugglers; but this I know, two parties have been to search, and found nothing but the bare walls of the tower. All is deserted by day, and dark by night; for no light was to be seen while we were there, though it burned sprightly enough when we were out at sea.'

'I have heard say,' observed the younger sailor, 'it is burned by the ghost of a maiden who lost her sweetheart in these parts; he being wrecked, and his body found at the foot of the tower. She goes by the name among us of the "Invisible Girl".'

The voyagers had now reached the landing place at the foot of the tower. Vernon cast a glance upwards – the light was still burning. With some difficulty, struggling with the breakers, and blinded by night, they contrived to get their little bark to shore, and to draw it up on the beach. They then scrambled up the precipitous pathway, overgrown by weeds and underwood, and, guided by the more experienced fishermen, they found the entrance to the tower, door or gate there was none, and all was dark as the tomb, and silent and almost as cold as death.

'This will never do,' said Vernon. 'Surely our hostess will show her light, if not herself, and guide our darkling steps by some sign of life and comfort.'

'We will get to the upper chamber,' said the sailor, 'if I can but hit upon the broken-down steps, but you will find no trace of the Invisible Girl nor her light either, I warrant.'

'Truly a romantic adventure of the most disagreeable kind,' muttered Vernon, as he stumbled over the unequal ground. 'She of the beacon light must be both ugly and old, or she would not be so peevish and inhospitable.'

With considerable difficulty, and after divers knocks and bruises, the adventurers at length succeeded in reaching the upper storey; but all was blank and bare, and they were fain to stretch themselves on the hard floor, when weariness, both of mind and body, conduced to steep their senses in sleep.

Long and sound were the slumbers of the mariners. Vernon but forgot himself for an hour; then, throwing off drowsiness, and finding his rough couch uncongenial to repose, he got up and placed himself at the hole that served for a window, for glass there was none, and there being not even a rough bench, he leaned his back against the embrasure, as the only rest he could find. He had forgotten his danger, the mysterious beacon and its invisible guardian: his thoughts were occupied on the horrors of his own fate, and the unspeakable wretchedness that sat like a nightmare on his heart.

It would require a good-sized volume to relate the causes which had changed the once happy Vernon into the most woeful mourner that ever clung to the outer trappings of grief, as slight though cherished symbols of the wretchedness within. Henry was the only child of Sir Peter Vernon, and as much spoiled by his father's idolatry as the old baronet's violent and tyrannical temper would permit. A young orphan was educated in his father's house, who in the same way was treated with generosity and kindness, and yet who lived in deep awe of Sir Peter's authority, who was a widower; and these two children were all he had to exert his power over, or to whom to extend his affection. Rosina was a cheerful-tempered girl, a little timid and careful to avoid displeasing her protector; but so docile, so kind-hearted and so affectionate, that she felt even less than Henry the discordant spirit of his parent. It is a tale often told; they were playmates and companions in childhood, and lovers in after days. Rosina was frightened to imagine that this secret affection, and the vows they pledged, might be disapproved of by Sir Peter. But sometimes she consoled herself by thinking that perhaps she was in reality her Henry's destined bride, brought up with him under the design of their future union; and Henry, while he felt that this was not the case, resolved to wait only until he was of age to declare and accomplish his wishes in making the sweet Rosina his wife. Meanwhile he was careful to avoid premature discovery of his intentions, so to secure his beloved girl from persecution and insult. The old gentleman was very conveniently blind; he lived always in the country, and the lovers spent their lives together, unrebuked and uncontrolled. It was enough that Rosina played on her mandolin, and sang Sir Peter to sleep every day after dinner; she was the sole female in the house above the rank of a servant, and had her own way in the disposal of her time.

Even when Sir Peter frowned, her innocent caresses and sweet voice were powerful to smooth the rough current of his temper. If ever human spirit lived in an earthly paradise, Rosina did at this time: her pure love was made happy by Henry's constant presence; and the confidence they felt in each other, and the security with which they looked forward to the future, rendered their path one of roses under a cloudless sky. Sir Peter was the slight drawback that only rendered their tête-à-tête more delightful, and gave value to the sympathy they each bestowed on the other. All at once an ominous personage made its appearance in Vernon Place, in the shape of a widow sister of Sir Peter, who, having succeeded in killing her husband and children with the effects of her vile temper, came, like a harpy, greedy for new prey, under her brother's roof. She, too soon, detected the attachment of the unsuspicious pair. She made all speed to impart her discovery to her brother, and at once to restrain and inflame his rage. Through her contrivance Henry was suddenly despatched on his travels abroad, that the coast might be clear for the persecution of Rosina; and then the richest of the lovely girl's many admirers, whom, under Sir Peter's single reign, she was allowed, nay, almost commanded, to dismiss, so desirous was he of keeping her for his own comfort, was selected, and she was ordered to marry him. The scenes of violence to which she was now exposed, the bitter taunts of the odious Mrs Bainbridge, and the reckless fury of Sir Peter, were the more frightful and overwhelming from their novelty. To all she could only oppose a silent, tearful, but immutable steadiness of purpose: no threats, no rage could extort from her more than a touching prayer that they would not hate her, because she could not obey.

'There must be something we don't see under all this,' said Mrs Bainbridge. 'Take my word for it, brother – she corresponds secretly with Henry. Let us take her down to your seat in Wales, where she will have no pensioned beggars to assist her; and we shall see if her spirit be not bent to our purpose.'

Sir Peter consented, and they all three posted down to — shire, and took up their abode in the solitary and dreary-looking house before alluded to as belonging to the family. Here poor Rosina's sufferings grew intolerable: before, surrounded by well-known scenes, and in perpetual intercourse with kind and familiar faces, she had not despaired in the end of conquering by her patience the cruelty of her persecutors; nor had she written to Henry, for his name had not been mentioned by his relatives, nor their attachment alluded to, and she felt an instinctive wish to escape the dangers about her without his being annoyed, or the sacred secret of her love being laid bare, and wronged by the vulgar abuse of his aunt or the bitter curses of his father. But when she was taken to Wales, and made a prisoner in her apartment, when the flinty mountains about her seemed feebly to imitate the stony hearts she had to deal with, her courage began to fail. The only attendant permitted to approach her was Mrs Bainbridge's maid; and under the tutelage of her fiend-like mistress, this woman was used as a decoy to entice the poor prisoner into confidence, and then to be betrayed. The simple, kind-hearted Rosina was a facile dupe, and at last, in the excess of her despair, wrote to Henry, and gave the letter to this woman to be forwarded. The letter in itself would have softened marble; it did not speak of their mutual vows, it but asked him to intercede with his father, that he would restore her to the kind place she had formerly held in his affections, and cease from a cruelty that would destroy her. 'For I may die,' wrote the hapless girl, 'but marry another – never!' That single word, indeed, had sufficed to betray her secret, had it not been already discovered; as it was, it gave increased fury to Sir Peter, as his sister triumphantly pointed it out to him, for it need hardly be said that while the ink of the address was yet wet, and the seal still warm, Rosina's letter was carried to this lady. The culprit was summoned before them. What ensued none could tell; for their own sakes the cruel pair tried to palliate their part. Voices were high, and the soft murmur of Rosina's tone was lost in the howling of Sir Peter and the snarling of his sister. 'Out of doors you shall go,' roared the old man. 'Under my roof you shall not spend another night.' And the words 'infamous seductress', and worse, such as had never met the poor girl's ear before, were caught by listening servants; and to each angry speech of the baronet, Mrs Bainbridge added an envenomed point worse than all.

More dead than alive, Rosina was at last dismissed. Whether guided by despair, whether she took Sir Peter's threats literally, or whether his sister's orders were more decisive, none knew, but Rosina left the house. A servant saw her cross the park, weeping and wringing her hands as she went. What became of her none could tell; her disappearance was not disclosed to Sir Peter till the following day, and then he showed, by his anxiety to trace her steps and to find her, that his words had been but idle threats. The truth was, that though Sir Peter went to frightful lengths to prevent the marriage of the heir of his house with the portionless orphan, the object of his charity, yet in his heart he loved Rosina, and half his violence to her rose from anger at himself for treating her so ill. Now remorse began to sting him, as messenger after messenger came back without tidings of his victim. He dared not confess his worst fears to himself; and when his inhuman sister, trying to harden her conscience by angry words, cried, 'The vile hussy has too surely made away with herself out of revenge to us,' an oath, the most tremendous, and a look sufficient to make even her tremble, commanded her silence. Her conjecture, however, appeared too true: a dark and rushing stream that flowed at the extremity of the park had doubtless received the lovely form, and quenched the life of this unfortunate girl. Sir Peter, when his endeavours to find her proved fruitless, returned to town, haunted by the image of his victim, and forced to acknowledge in his own heart that he would willingly lay down his life, could he see her again, even though it were as the bride of his son – his son, before whose questioning he quailed like the veriest coward. For when Henry was told of the death of Rosina, he suddenly returned from abroad to ask the cause – to visit her grave, and mourn her loss in the groves and valleys which had been the scenes of their mutual happiness. He made a thousand enquiries, and an ominous silence alone replied. Growing more earnest and more anxious, at length he drew from servants and dependants, and his odious aunt herself, the whole dreadful truth. From that moment despair struck his heart, and misery named him her own. He fled from his father's presence; and the recollection that one whom he ought to revere was guilty of so dark a crime, haunted him, as of old the Eumenides tormented the souls of men given up to their torturings. His first, his only wish, was to visit Wales, and to learn if any new discovery had been made, and whether it were possible to recover the mortal remains of the lost Rosina, so to satisfy the unquiet longings of his miserable heart. On this expedition was he bound, when he made his appearance at the village before named; and now in the deserted tower, his thoughts were busy with images of despair and death, and what his beloved one had suffered before her gentle nature had been goaded to such a deed of woe.

While immersed in gloomy reverie, to which the monotonous roaring of the sea made fit accompaniment, hours flew on, and Vernon was at last aware that the light of morning was creeping from out its eastern retreat, and dawning over the wild ocean, which still broke in furious tumult on the rocky beach. His companions now roused themselves, and prepared to depart. The food they had brought with them was damaged by sea water, and their hunger, after hard labour and many hours fasting, had become ravenous. It was impossible to put to sea in their shattered boat; but there stood a fisher's cot about two miles off, in a recess in the bay, of which the promontory on which the tower stood formed one side, and to this they hastened to repair. They did not spend a second thought on the light which had saved them, nor its cause, but left the ruin in search of a more hospitable asylum. Vernon cast his eyes round as he quitted it, but no vestige of an inhabitant met his eye, and he began to persuade himself that the beacon had been a creation of fancy merely. Arriving at the cottage in question, which was inhabited by a fisherman and his family, they made a homely breakfast, and then prepared to return to the tower, to refit their boat, and if possible bring her round. Vernon accompanied them, together with their host and his son. Several questions were asked concerning the Invisible Girl and her light, each agreeing that the apparition was novel, and not one being able to give even an explanation of how the name had become affixed to the unknown cause of this singular appearance; though both of the men of the cottage affirmed that once or twice they had seen a female figure in the adjacent wood, and that now and then a stranger girl made her appearance at another cot a mile off, on the other side of the promontory, and bought bread; they suspected both these to be the same, but could not tell. The inhabitants of the cot, indeed, appeared too stupid even to feel curiosity, and had never made any attempt at discovery. The whole day was spent by the sailors in repairing the boat; and the sound of hammers, and the voices of the men at work, resounded along the coast, mingled with the dashing of the waves. This was no time to explore the ruin for one who whether human or supernatural so evidently withdrew herself from intercourse with every living being. Vernon, however, went over the tower, and searched every nook in vain; the dingy bare walls bore no token of serving as a shelter; and even a little recess in the wall of the staircase, which he had not before observed, was equally empty and desolate. Quitting the tower, he wandered in the pine wood that surrounded it, and giving up all thought of solving the mystery, was soon engrossed by thoughts that touched his heart more nearly, when suddenly there appeared on the ground at his feet the vision of a slipper. Since Cinderella so tiny a slipper had never been seen; as plain as shoe could speak, it told a tale of elegance, loveliness and youth. Vernon picked it up; he had often admired Rosina's singularly small foot, and his first thought was a question whether this little slipper would have fitted it. It was very strange! It must belong to the Invisible Girl. Then there was a fairy form that kindled that light, a form of such material substance, that its foot needed to be shod; and yet how shod? With kid so fine, and of shape so exquisite, that it exactly resembled such as Rosina wore! Again the recurrence of the image of the beloved dead came forcibly across him; and a thousand home-felt associations, childish yet sweet, and lover-like though trifling, so filled Vernon's heart, that he threw himself his length on the ground, and wept more bitterly than ever the miserable fate of the sweet orphan.

In the evening the men quitted their work, and Vernon returned with them to the cot where they were to sleep, intending to pursue their voyage, weather permitting, the following morning. Vernon said nothing of his slipper, but returned with his rough associates. Often he looked back; but the tower rose darkly over the dim waves, and no light appeared. Preparations had been made in the cot for their accommodation, and the only bed in it was offered Vernon; but he refused to deprive his hostess, and, spreading his cloak on a heap of dry leaves, endeavoured to give himself up to repose. He slept for some hours; and when he awoke, all was still, save that the hard breathing of the sleepers in the same room with him interrupted the silence. He rose, and going to the window, looked out over the now placid sea towards the mystic tower; the light burning there, sending its slender rays across the waves. Congratulating himself on a circumstance he had not anticipated, Vernon softly left the cottage, and, wrapping his cloak round him, walked with a swift pace round the bay towards the tower. He reached it; still the light was burning. To enter and restore the maiden her shoe, would be but an act of courtesy; and Vernon intended to do this with such caution, as to come unaware, before its wearer could, with her accustomed arts, withdraw herself from his eyes; but, unluckily, while yet making his way up the narrow pathway, his foot dislodged a loose fragment that fell with crash and sound down the precipice. He sprung forward, on this, to retrieve by speed the advantage he had lost by this unlucky accident. He reached the door. He entered: all was silent, but also all was dark. He paused in the room below; he felt sure that a slight sound met his ear. He ascended the steps, and entered the upper chamber; but blank obscurity met his penetrating gaze, the starless night admitted not even a twilight glimmer through the only aperture. He closed his eyes, to try, on opening them again, to be able to catch some faint, wandering ray on the visual nerve; but it was in vain. He groped round the room. He stood still, and held his breath; and then, listening intently, he felt sure that another occupied the chamber with him, and that its atmosphere was slightly agitated by another's respiration. He remembered the recess in the staircase; but, before he approached it, he spoke. He hesitated a moment what to say. 'I must believe,' he said, 'that misfortune alone can cause your seclusion; and if the assistance of a man – of a gentleman –'

An exclamation interrupted him; a voice from the grave spoke his name – the accents of Rosina syllabled, 'Henry! Is it indeed Henry whom I hear?'

He rushed forward, directed by the sound, and clasped in his arms the living form of his own lamented girl – his own Invisible Girl he called her; for even yet, as he felt her heart beat near his, and as he entwined her waist with his arm, supporting her as she almost sank to the ground with agitation, he could not see her; and, as her sobs prevented her speech, no sense, but the instinctive one that filled his heart with tumultuous gladness, told him that the slender, wasted form he pressed so fondly was the living shadow of the Hebe beauty he had adored.

The morning saw this pair thus strangely restored to each other on the tranquil sea, sailing with a fair wind for L—, whence they were to proceed to Sir Peter's seat, which, three months before, Rosina had quitted in such agony and terror. The morning light dispelled the shadows that had veiled her, and disclosed the fair person of the Invisible Girl. Altered indeed she was by suffering and woe, but still the same sweet smile played on her lips, and the tender light of her soft blue eyes were all her own. Vernon drew out the slipper, and showed the cause that had occasioned him to resolve to discover the guardian of the mystic beacon; even now he dared not enquire how she had existed in that desolate spot, or wherefore she had so sedulously avoided observation, when the right thing to have been done was to have sought him immediately, under whose care, protected by whose love, no danger need be feared. But Rosina shrank from him as he spoke, and a death-like pallor came over her cheek, as she faintly whispered, 'Your father's curse – your father's dreadful threats!' It appeared, indeed, that Sir Peter's violence, and the cruelty of Mrs Bainbridge, had succeeded in impressing Rosina with wild and unvanquishable terror. She had fled from their house without plan or forethought – driven by frantic horror and overwhelming fear, she had left it with scarcely any money, and there seemed to her no possibility of either returning or proceeding onwards. She had no friend except Henry in the wide world; whither could she go? To have sought Henry would have sealed their fates to misery; for, with an oath, Sir Peter had declared he would rather see them both in their coffins than married. After wandering about, hiding by day, and only venturing forth at night, she had come to this deserted tower, which seemed a place of refuge. How she had lived since then she could hardly tell. She had lingered in the woods by day, or slept in the vault of the tower, an asylum none were acquainted with or had discovered. By night she burned the pine-cones of the wood, and night was her dearest time; for it seemed to her as if security came with darkness. She was unaware that Sir Peter had left that part of the country, and was terrified lest her hiding place should be revealed to him. Her only hope was that Henry would return – that Henry would never rest till he had found her. She confessed that the long interval and the approach of winter had visited her with dismay; she feared, as her strength was failing, and her form wasting to a skeleton, that she might die, and never see her own Henry more.

An illness, indeed, in spite of all his care, followed her restoration to security and the comforts of civilised life. Many months went by before the bloom revisiting her cheeks, and her limbs regaining their roundness, she resembled once more the picture drawn of her in her days of bliss, before any visitation of sorrow. It was a copy of this portrait that decorated the tower, the scene of her suffering, in which I had found shelter. Sir Peter, overjoyed to be relieved from the pangs of remorse, and delighted again to see his orphan-ward, whom he really loved, was now as eager as before he had been averse to bless her union with his son. Mrs Bainbridge they never saw again. But each year they spent a few months in their Welsh mansion, the scene of their early wedded happiness, and the spot where again poor Rosina had awoken to life and joy after her cruel persecutions. Henry's fond care had fitted up the tower, and decorated it as I saw; and often did he come over, with his 'Invisible Girl', to renew, in the very scene of its occurrence, the remembrance of all the incidents which had led to their meeting again, during the shades of night, in that sequestered ruin.

THE MOURNER

One fatal remembrance, one sorrow that throws
Its bleak shade alike o'er our joys and our woes,
To which life nothing darker or brighter can bring,
For which joy has no balm, and affliction no sting!

A gorgeous scene of kingly pride is the prospect now before us! The offspring of art, the nursling of nature – where can the eye rest on a landscape more deliciously lovely than the fair expanse of Virginia Water, now an open mirror to the sky, now shaded by umbrageous banks, which wind into dark recesses, or are rounded into soft promontories? Looking down on it, now that the sun is low in the west, the eye is dazzled, the soul oppressed, by excess of beauty. Earth, water, air, drink to overflowing the radiance that streams from yonder well of light: the foliage of the trees seems dripping with the golden flood; while the lake, filled with no earthly dew, appears but an imbasining of the sun-tinctured atmosphere; and trees and gay pavilion float in its depth, more clear, more distinct, than their twins in the upper air. Nor is the scene silent: strains more sweet than those that lull Venus to her balmy rest, more inspiring than the song of Tiresias which awoke Alexander to the deed of ruin, more solemn than the chantings of St Cecilia, float along the waves and mingle with the lagging breeze, which ruffles not the lake. Strange, that a few dark scores should be the key to this fountain of sound; the unconscious link between unregarded noise, and harmonies which unclose paradise to our entranced senses!

The sun touches the extreme boundary, and a softer, milder light mingles a roseate tinge with the fiery glow. Our boat has floated long on the broad expanse; now let it approach the umbrageous bank. The green tresses of the graceful willow dip into the waters, which are checked by them into a ripple. The startled teal dart from their recess, skimming the waves with splashing wing. The stately swans float onwards; while innumerable water fowl cluster together out of the way of the oars. The twilight is blotted by no dark shades; it is one subdued, equal receding of the great tide of day, which leaves the shingles bare, but not deformed. We may disembark and wander yet amid the glades, long before the thickening shadows speak of night. The plantations are formed of every English tree, with an old oak or two standing out in the walks. There the glancing foliage obscures heaven, as the silken texture of a veil a woman's lovely features. Beneath such fretwork we may indulge in light-hearted thoughts; or, if sadder meditations lead us to seek darker shades, we may pass the cascade towards the large groves of pine, with their vast undergrowth of laurel, reaching up to the Belvedere; or, on the opposite side of the water, sit under the shadow of the silverstemmed birch, or beneath the leafy pavilions of those fine old beeches, whose high fantastic roots seem formed in nature's sport; and the near jungle of sweet-smelling myrica leaves no sense unvisited by pleasant ministration.

Now this splendid scene is reserved for the royal possessor; but in past years, while the lodge was called the Regent's Cottage, or before, when the under ranger inhabited it, the mazy paths of Chapel Wood were open, and the iron gates enclosing the plantations and Virginia Water were guarded by no Cerberus untamable by sops. It was here, on a summer's evening, that Horace Neville and his two fair cousins floated idly on the placid lake,

In that sweet mood when pleasant thoughts
Bring sad thoughts to the mind.

Neville had been eloquent in praise of English scenery. 'In distant climes,' he said, 'we may find landscapes grand in barbaric wildness, or rich in the luxuriant vegetation of the south, or sublime in Alpine magnificence. We may lament, though it is ungrateful to say so on such a night as this, the want of a more genial sky; but where find scenery to be compared to the verdant, well-wooded, well-watered groves of our native land; the clustering cottages, shadowed by fine old elms; each garden blooming with early flowers, each lattice gay with geraniums and roses; the blue-eyed child devouring his white bread, while he drives a cow to graze; the hedge redolent with summer blooms; the enclosed cornfields, seas of golden grain, weltering in the breeze; the stile, the track across the meadow, leading through the copse, under which the path winds, and the meeting branches overhead, which give, by their dimming tracery, a cathedral-like solemnity to the scene; the river, winding "with sweet inland murmur"; and, as additional graces, spots like these – oases of taste – gardens of Eden – the works of wealth, which evince at once the greatest power and the greatest will to create beauty?

'And yet,' continued Neville, 'it was with difficulty that I persuaded myself to reap the best fruits of my uncle's will, and to inhabit this spot, familiar to my boyhood, associated with unavailing regrets and recollected pain.'

Horace Neville was a man of birth – of wealth; but he could hardly be termed a man of the world. There was in his nature a gentleness, a sweetness, a winning sensibility, allied to talent and personal distinction, that gave weight to his simplest expressions, and excited sympathy for all his emotions. His younger cousin, his junior by several years, was attached to him by the tenderest sentiments – secret long – but they were now betrothed to each other – a lovely, happy pair. She looked enquiringly; but he turned away. 'No more of this,' he said, and giving a swifter impulse to their boat, they speedily reached the shore, landed, and walked through the long extent of Chapel Wood. It was dark night before they met their carriage at Bishopsgate.

A week or two after, Horace received letters to call him to a distant part of the country: it even seemed possible that he might be obliged to visit an estate in the north of Ireland. A few days before his departure, he requested his cousin to walk with him. They bent their steps across several meadows to Old Windsor churchyard. At first he did not deviate from the usual path; and as they went they talked cheerfully, gaily. The beauteous sunny day might well exhilarate them: the dancing waves sped onwards at their feet, the country church lifted its rustic spire into the bright pure sky. There was nothing in their conversation that could induce his cousin to think that Neville had led her hither for any saddening purpose. But when they were about to quit the churchyard, Horace, as if he had suddenly recollected himself, turned from the path, crossed the greensward, and paused beside a grave near the river. No stone was there to commemorate the being who reposed beneath – it was thickly grown with rich grass, starred by a luxuriant growth of humble daisies; a few dead leaves, a broken bramble twig, defaced its neatness. Neville removed these, and then said, 'Juliet, I commit this sacred spot to your keeping while I am away.'

'There is no monument,' he continued, 'for her commands were implicitly obeyed by the two beings to whom she addressed them. One day another may lie near, and his name will be her epitaph. I do not mean myself,' he said, half smiling at the terror his cousin's countenance expressed. 'But promise me, Juliet, to preserve this grave from every violation. I do not wish to sadden you by the story; yet, if I have excited your curiosity – your interest, I should say – I will satisfy it; but not now – not here.'

Leaving the churchyard, they found their horses in attendance, and they prolonged their ride across Bishopsgate Heath. Neville's mind was full of the events to which he had alluded: he began the tale, and then abruptly broke off. It was not till the following day, when, in company with her sister, they again visited Virginia Water, that, seated under the shadow of its pines, whose melodious swinging in the wind breathed unearthly harmony, and looking down upon the water, association of place, and its extreme beauty, reviving, yet soothing, the recollections of the past, unasked by his companions, Neville at once commenced his story.

'I was sent to Eton at eleven years of age. I will not dwell upon my sufferings there; I would hardly refer to them, did they not make a part of my present narration. I was a fag to a hard taskmaster; every labour he could invent – and the youthful tyrant was ingenious – he devised for my annoyance; early and late, I was forced to be in attendance, to the neglect of my school duties, so incurring punishment. There were worse things to bear than these: it was his delight to put me to shame, and – finding that I had too much of my mother in my blood – to endeavour to compel me to acts of cruelty from which my nature revolted. I refused to obey. Speak of West Indian slavery! I hope things may be better now; in my days, the tender years of aristocratic childhood were yielded up to a capricious, unrelenting, cruel bondage, far beyond the measured despotism of Jamaica.

'One day – I had been two years at school, and was nearly thirteen – my tyrant, I will give him no other name, issued a command, in the wantonness of power, for me to destroy a poor little bullfinch I had tamed and caged. In a hapless hour he found it in my room, and was indignant that I should dare to appropriate a single pleasure. I refused, stubbornly, dauntlessly, though the consequence of my disobedience was immediate and terrible. At this moment a message came from my tormentor's tutor – his father had arrived. 'Well, old lad,' he cried, 'I shall pay you off some day!' Seizing my pet at the same time, he wrung its neck, threw it at my feet, and, with a laugh of derision, quitted the room.

'Never before – never may I again feel the same swelling, boiling fury in my bursting heart. The sight of my nursling expiring at my feet, my desire of vengeance, my impotence, created a Vesuvius within me that no tears flowed to quench. Could I have uttered – acted – my passion, it would have been less torturous: it was so when I burst into a torrent of abuse and imprecation. My vocabulary – it must have been a choice collection – was supplied by him against whom it was levelled. But words were air. I desired to give more substantial proof of my resentment. I destroyed everything in the room belonging to him; I tore them to pieces, I stamped on them, crushed them with more than childish strength. My last act was to seize a timepiece, on which my tyrant infinitely prided himself, and to dash it to the ground. The sight of this, as it lay shattered at my feet, recalled me to my senses, and something like an emotion of fear allayed the tumult in my heart. I began to meditate an escape. I got out of the house, ran down a lane and across some meadows, far out of bounds, above Eton. I was seen by an older boy, a friend of my tormentor. He called to me, thinking at first that I was performing some errand for him; but seeing that I shirked, he repeated his "*Come up!*" in an authoritative voice. It put wings to my heels; he did not deem it necessary to pursue. But I grow tedious, my dear

Juliet; enough that fears the most intense, of punishment both from my masters and the upper boys, made me resolve to run away. I reached the banks of the Thames, tied my clothes over my head, swam across, and, traversing several fields, entered Windsor Forest, with a vague childish feeling of being able to hide myself for ever in the unexplored obscurity of its immeasurable wilds. It was early autumn; the weather was mild, even warm; the forest oaks yet showed no sign of winter change, though the fern beneath wore a yellowy tinge. I got within Chapel Wood; I fed upon chestnuts and beechnuts; I continued to hide myself from the gamekeepers and wood-men. I lived thus two days.

'But chestnuts and beechnuts were sorry fare to a growing lad of thirteen years old. A day's rain occurred, and I began to think myself the most unfortunate boy on record. I had a distant, obscure idea of starvation. I thought of the *Children in the Wood*, of their leafy shroud, gift of the pious robin; this brought my poor bullfinch to my mind, and tears streamed in torrents down my cheeks. I thought of my father and mother; of you, then my little baby cousin and playmate; and I cried with renewed fervour, till, quite exhausted, I curled myself up under a huge oak among some dry leaves, the relics of a hundred summers, and fell asleep.

'I ramble on in my narration as if I had a story to tell, yet I have little except a portrait – a sketch – to present, for your amusement or interest. When I awoke, the first object that met my opening eyes was a little foot, delicately clad in silk and soft kid. I looked up in dismay, expecting to behold some gaily dressed appendage to this indication of high-bred elegance; but I saw a girl, perhaps seventeen, simply clad in a dark cotton dress, her face shaded by a large very coarse straw hat. She was pale even to marmoreal whiteness; her chestnut-coloured hair was parted in plain tresses across a brow which wore traces of extreme suffering; her eyes were blue, full, large, melancholy, often even suffused with tears; but her mouth had an infantine sweetness and innocence in its expression, that softened the otherwise sad expression of her countenance.

'She spoke to me. I was too hungry, too exhausted, too unhappy, to resist her kindness, and gladly permitted her to lead me to her home. We passed out of the wood by some broken palings on to Bishopsgate Heath, and after no long walk arrived at her habitation. It was a solitary, dreary-looking cottage; the palings were in disrepair, the garden waste, the lattices unadorned by flowers or creepers; within, all was neat, but sombre, and even mean. The diminutiveness of a cottage requires an appearance of cheerfulness and elegance to make it pleasing; the bare floor – clean, it is true – the rush chairs, deal table, checked curtains of this cot, were beneath even a peasant's rusticity; yet it was the dwelling of my lovely guide, whose little white hand, delicately gloved, contrasted with her unadorned attire, as did her gentle self with the clumsy appurtenances of her too humble dwelling.

'Poor child! She had meant entirely to hide her origin, to degrade herself to a peasant's state, and little thought that she for ever betrayed herself by the strangest incongruities. Thus, the arrangements of her table were mean, her fare meagre for a hermit; but the linen was matchlessly fine, and wax lights stood in candlesticks which a beggar would almost have disdained to own. But I talk of circumstances I observed afterwards; then I was chiefly aware of the plentiful breakfast she caused her single attendant, a young girl, to place before me, and of the sweet soothing voice of my hostess, which spoke a kindness with which lately I had been little conversant. When my hunger was appeased, she drew my story from me, encouraged me to write to my father, and kept me at her abode till, after a few days, I returned to school pardoned. No long time elapsed before I got into the upper forms, and my woeful slavery ended.

'Whenever I was able, I visited my disguised nymph. I no longer associated with my schoolfellows; their diversions, their pursuits, appeared vulgar and stupid to me. I had but one object in view – to accomplish my lessons, and to steal to the cottage of Ellen Burnet.

'Do not look grave, love! True, others as young as I then was have loved, and I might also; but not Ellen. Her profound, her intense melancholy, sister to despair – her serious, sad discourse – her mind, estranged from all worldly concerns, forbade that; but there was an enchantment in her sorrow, a fascination in her converse, that lifted me above commonplace existence. She created a magic circle, which I entered as holy ground. It was not akin to heaven, for grief was the presiding spirit; but there was an exaltation of sentiment, an enthusiasm, a view beyond the grave, which made it unearthly, singular, wild, enthralling. You have often observed that I strangely differ from all other men; I mingle with them, make one in their occupations and diversions, but I have a portion of my being sacred from them. A living well, sealed up from their contamination, lies deep in my heart – it is of little use, but there it is; Ellen opened the spring, and it has flowered ever since.

'Of what did she talk? She recited no past adventures, alluded to no past intercourse with friend or relative; she spoke of the various woes that wait on humanity, on the intricate mazes of life, on the miseries of passion, of love, remorse and death, and that which we may hope or fear beyond the tomb; she spoke of the sensation of wretchedness alive in her own broken heart, and then she grew fearfully eloquent, till, suddenly pausing, she reproached herself for making me familiar with such wordless misery. "I do you harm," she often said. "I unfit you for society. I have tried, seeing you thrown upon yonder distorted miniature of a bad world, to estrange you from its evil contagion. I fear that I shall be the cause of greater harm to you than could spring from association with your fellow creatures in the ordinary course of things. This is not well – avoid the stricken deer."

'There were darker shades in the picture than those which I have already developed. Ellen was more miserable than the imagination of one like you, dear girl, unacquainted with woe, can portray. Sometimes she gave words to her despair – it was so great as to confuse the boundary between physical and mental sensation – and every pulsation of her heart was a throb of pain. She has suddenly broken off in talking of her sorrows, with a cry of agony – bidding me leave her – hiding her face on her arms, shivering with the anguish some thought awoke. The idea that chiefly haunted her, though she earnestly endeavoured to put it aside, was self-destruction – to snap the silver cord that bound together so much grace, wisdom and sweetness – to rob the world of a creation made to be its ornament. Sometimes her piety checked her; oftener a sense of unendurable suffering made her brood with pleasure over the dread resolve. She spoke of it to me as being wicked; yet I often fancied this was done rather to prevent her example from being of ill effect to me, than from any conviction that the Father of all would regard angrily the last act of his miserable child. Once she had prepared the mortal beverage; it was on the table before her when I entered. She did not deny its nature, she did not attempt to justify herself; she only besought me not to hate her and to soothe by my kindness her last moments. "I cannot live!" was all her explanation, all her excuse; and it was spoken with such fervent wretchedness that it seemed wrong to attempt to persuade her to prolong the sense of pain. I did not act like a boy – I wonder I did not – I made one simple request, to which she instantly acceded, that she should walk with me to this Belvedere. It was a glorious sunset; beauty and the spirit of love breathed in the wind, and hovered over the softened hues of the landscape. "Look, Ellen," I cried, "if only such loveliness of nature existed, it were worth living for!"

'"True, if a latent feeling did not blot this glorious scene with murky shadows. Beauty is as we see it – my eyes view all things deformed and evil." She closed them as she said this; but, young and sensitive, the visitings of the soft breeze already began to minister consolation. "Dearest Ellen," I continued, "what do I not owe to you? I am your boy, your pupil. I might have gone on blindly as others do, but you opened my eyes; you have given me a sense of the just, the good, the beautiful – and have you done this merely for my misfortune? If you leave me, what can become of me?" The last words came from my heart, and tears gushed from my eyes. "Do not leave me, Ellen," I said. "I cannot live without you – and I cannot die, for I have a mother – a father." She turned quickly round, saying, "You are blessed sufficiently." Her voice struck me as unnatural; she grew deadly pale as she spoke, and was obliged to sit down. Still I clung to her, prayed, cried, till she – I had never seen her shed a tear before – burst into passionate weeping. After this she seemed to forget her resolve. We returned by moonlight, and our talk was even more calm and cheerful than usual. When in her cottage, I poured away the fatal draught. Her "goodnight" bore with it no traces of her late agitation; and the next day she said, "I have thoughtlessly, even wickedly, created a new duty to myself, even at a time when I had forsworn all; but I will be true to it. Pardon me for making you familiar with emotions and scenes so dire. I will behave better – I will preserve myself, if I can, till the link between us is loosened, or broken, and I am free again."

'One little incident alone occurred during our intercourse that appeared at all to connect her with the world. Sometimes I brought her a newspaper, for those were stirring times; and though, before I knew her, she had forgotten all except the world her own heart enclosed, yet, to please me, she would talk of Napoleon, Russia – from whence the emperor now returned overthrown – and the prospect of his final defeat. The paper lay one day on her table; some words caught her eye; she bent eagerly down to read them, and her bosom heaved with violent palpitation; but she subdued herself, and after a few moments told me to take the paper away. Then, indeed, I did feel an emotion of even impertinent inquisitiveness. I found nothing to satisfy it – though afterwards I became aware that it contained a singular advertisement, saying, "If these lines meet the eye of any one of the passengers who were on board the *St Mary*, bound for Liverpool from Barbados, which sailed on the third of May last, and was destroyed by fire in the high seas, a part of the crew only having been saved by His Majesty's frigate the *Bellerophon*, they are entreated to communicate with the advertiser: and if any one be acquainted with the particulars of the Hon. Miss Eversham's fate and present abode, they are earnestly requested to disclose them, directing to L.E., Stratton Street, Park Lane."

'It was after this event, as winter came on, that symptoms of decided ill health declared themselves in the delicate frame of my poor Ellen. I have often suspected that, without positively attempting her life, she did many things that tended to abridge it and to produce mortal disease. Now, when really ill, she refused all medical attendance; but she got better again, and I thought her nearly well when I saw her for the last time, before going home for the Christmas holidays. Her manner was full of affection: she relied, she said, on the continuation of my friendship. She made me promise never to forget her, though she refused to write to me, and forbade any letters from me.

'Even now I see her standing at her humble doorway. If an appearance of illness and suffering can ever be termed lovely, it was in her. Still she was to be viewed as the wreck of beauty. What must she not have been in happier days, with her angel expression of face, her nymph-like figure, her voice, whose tones were music? "So young – so lost!" was the sentiment that burst even from me, a young lad, as I waved my hand to her as a last adieu. She hardly looked more than fifteen, but none could doubt that her very soul was impressed by the sad lines of sorrow that rested so unceasingly on her fair brow. Away from her, her figure for ever floated before my eyes. I put my hands before them, still she was there: my day, my night, dreams were filled by my recollections of her.

'During the winter holidays, on a fine soft day, I went out to hunt. You, dear Juliet, will remember the sad catastrophe: I fell and broke my leg. The only person who saw me fall was a young man who rode one of the most beautiful horses I ever saw, and I believe it was by watching him as he took a leap that I incurred my disaster. He dismounted, and was at my side in a minute. My own animal had fled. He called his. It obeyed his voice. With ease he lifted my light figure on to the saddle, contriving to support my leg, and so conducted me a short distance to a lodge situated in the woody recesses of Elmore Park, the seat of the Earl of D—, whose second son my preserver was. He was my sole nurse for a day or two, and during the whole of my illness passed many hours of each day by my bedside. As I lay gazing on him, while he read to me, or talked, narrating a thousand strange adventures which had occurred during his service in the Peninsula, I thought – is it for ever to be my fate to fall in with the highly gifted and excessively unhappy?

'The immediate neighbour of Lewis' family was Lord Eversham. He had married in very early youth, and became a widower young. After this misfortune, which passed like a deadly blight over his prospects and possessions, leaving the gay view utterly sterile and bare, he left his surviving infant daughter under the care of Lewis' mother, and travelled for many years in far distant lands. He returned when Clarice was about ten, a lovely sweet child, the pride and delight of all connected with her. Lord Eversham, on his return – he was then hardly more than thirty – devoted himself to her education. They were never separate: he was a good musician, and she became a proficient under his tutoring. They rode, walked, read together. When a father is all that a father may be, the sentiments of filial piety, entire dependence and perfect confidence being united, the love of a daughter is one of the deepest and strongest, as it is the purest passion of which our natures are capable. Clarice worshipped her parent, who came, during the transition from mere childhood to the period when reflection and observation awaken, to adorn a commonplace existence with all the brilliant adjuncts which enlightened and devoted affection can bestow. He appeared to her like an especial gift of Providence, a guardian angel – but far dearer, as being akin to her own nature. She grew, under his eye, in loveliness and refinement both of intellect and heart. These feelings were not divided – almost strengthened, by the engagement that had place between her and Lewis. Lewis was destined for the army, and, after a few years' service, they were to be united.

'It is hard, when all is fair and tranquil, when the world, opening before the ardent gaze of youth, looks like a well-kept demesne, unencumbered by let or hindrance for the annoyance of the young traveller, that we should voluntarily stray into desert wilds and tempest-visited districts. Lewis Elmore was ordered to Spain; and, at the same time, Lord Eversham found it necessary to visit some estates he possessed in Barbados. He was not sorry to revisit a scene, which had dwelt in his memory as an earthly paradise, nor to show to his daughter a new and strange world, so to form her understanding and enlarge her mind. They were to return in three months, and departed as on a summer tour. Clarice was glad that, while her lover gathered experience and knowledge in a distant land, she should not remain in idleness; she was glad that there would be some diversion for her anxiety during his perilous absence; and in every way she enjoyed the idea of travelling with her beloved father, who would fill every hour, and adorn every new scene, with pleasure and delight. They sailed. Clarice wrote home, with enthusiastic expressions of rapture and delight, from Madeira. Yet, without her father, she said, the fair scene had been blank to her. More than half her letter was filled by the expressions of her gratitude and affection for her adored and revered parent. While he, in his, with fewer words, perhaps, but with no less energy, spoke of his satisfaction in her improvement, his pride in her beauty, and his grateful sense of her love and kindness.

'Such were they, a matchless example of happiness in the dearest connection in life, as resulting from the exercise of their reciprocal duties and affections. A father and daughter:

the one all care, gentleness and sympathy, consecrating his life for her happiness; the other, fond, duteous, grateful. Such had they been – and where were they now, the noble, kind, respected parent, and the beloved and loving child? They had departed from England as on a pleasure voyage down an inland stream, but the ruthless car of destiny had overtaken them on their unsuspecting way, crushing them under its heavy wheels – scattering love, hope and joy, as the bellowing avalanche overwhelms and grinds to mere spray the streamlet of the valley. They were gone: but whither? Mystery hung over the fate of the most helpless victim; and my friend's anxiety was to penetrate the clouds that hid poor Clarice from his sight.

'After an absence of a few months, they had written, fixing their departure in the *St Mary*, to sail from Barbados in a few days. Lewis, at the same time, returned from Spain. He was invalided, in his very first action, by a bad wound in his side. He arrived, and each day expected to hear of the landing of his friends; when that common messenger, the newspaper, brought him tidings to fill him with more than anxiety – with fear and agonising doubt. The *St Mary* had caught fire and had burned in the open sea. A frigate, the *Bellerophon*, had saved a part of the crew. In spite of illness and a physician's commands, Lewis set out the same day for London, to ascertain as speedily as possible the fate of her he loved. There he heard that the frigate was expected in the Downs. Without alighting from his travelling chaise, he posted thither, arriving in a burning fever. He went on board, saw the commander and spoke with the crew. They could give him few particulars as to whom they had saved: they had touched at Liverpool, and left there most of the persons, including all the passengers rescued from the *St Mary*. Physical suffering for awhile disabled

Mr Elmore; he was confined by his wound and consequent fever, and only recovered to give himself up to his exertions to discover the fate of his friends. They did not appear nor write; and all Lewis' enquiries only tended to confirm his worst fears. Yet still he hoped, and still continued indefatigable in his perquisitions. He visited Liverpool and Ireland, whither some of the passengers had gone, and learned only scattered, incongruous details of the fearful tragedy, that told nothing of Miss Eversham's present abode; though much that confirmed his suspicion that she still lived.

'The fire on board the *St Mary* had raged long and fearfully before the *Bellerophon* hove in sight, and boats came off for the rescue of the crew. The women were to be first embarked; but Clarice clung to her father, and refused to go till he should accompany her. Some fearful presentiment that, if she were saved, he would remain and die, gave such energy to her resolve, that not the entreaties of her father, nor the angry expostulations of the captain, could shake it. Lewis saw this man, after the lapse of two or three months, and he threw most light on the dark scene. He well remembered that, transported with anger by her woman's obstinacy, he had said to her, "You will cause your father's death – and be as much a parricide as if you put poison into his cup – you are not the first girl who has murdered her father in her wilful mood." Still Clarice passionately refused to go – there was no time for long parley – the point was yielded and she remained pale, but firm, near her parent, whose arm was around her, supporting her during the awful interval. It was no period for regular action and calm order: a tempest was rising, the scorching flames blew this way and that, making a fearful day of the night which veiled all except the burning ship. The boats returned with difficulty, and one only could contrive to approach; it was nearly full.

Lord Eversham and his daughter advanced to the deck's edge, to get in. "We can only take one of you," vociferated the sailors. "Keep back on your life! Throw the girl to us – we will come back for you if we can." Lord Eversham cast with a strong arm his daughter, who had now entirely lost her self-possession, into the boat. She was alive again in a minute, she called to her father, held out her arms to him, and would have thrown herself into the sea, but was held back by the sailors. Meanwhile Lord Eversham feeling that no boat could again approach the lost vessel, contrived to heave a spar overboard, and threw himself into the sea, clinging to it. The boat, tossed by the huge waves, with difficulty made its way to the frigate; and as it rose from the trough of the sea, Clarice saw her father struggling with his fate – battling with the death that at last became the victor. The spar floated by – his arms had fallen from it; were those his pallid features? She neither wept nor fainted, but her limbs grew rigid, her face colourless, and she was lifted as a log on to the deck of the frigate.

'The captain allowed that on her homeward voyage, the people had rather a horror of her, as having caused her father's death. Her own servants had perished; few people remembered who she was, but they talked together with no careful voices as they passed her, and a hundred times she must have heard herself accused of having destroyed her parent. She spoke to no one, or only in brief reply when addressed; to avoid the rough remonstrances of those around, she appeared at table, ate as well as she could; but there was a settled wretchedness in her face that never changed. When they landed at Liverpool, the captain conducted her to a hotel. He left her, meaning to return, but an opportunity of sailing that night for the Downs occurred, of which he availed himself, without again visiting her. He knew, he said, and truly, that she was in her native country, where she had but to write a letter to gather crowds of friends about her; and where can greater civility be found than at an English hotel, if it is known that you are perfectly able to pay your bill?

'This was all that Mr Elmore could learn, and it took many months to gather together these few particulars. He went to the hotel at Liverpool. It seemed that as soon as there appeared some hope of rescue from the frigate, Lord Eversham had given his pocketbook to his daughter's care, containing bills on a banking house at Liverpool to the amount of a few hundred pounds. On the second day after Clarice's arrival there, she had sent for the master of the hotel, and showed him these. He got the cash for her; and the next day she quitted Liverpool in a little coasting vessel. In vain Lewis endeavoured to trace her. Apparently she had crossed to Ireland; but whatever she had done, wherever she had gone, she had taken infinite pains to conceal, and all clue was speedily lost.

'Lewis had not yet despaired; he was even now perpetually making journeys, sending emissaries, employing every possible means for her discovery. From the moment he told me this story, we talked of nothing else. I became deeply interested, and we ceaselessly discussed the probabilities of the case, and where she might be concealed. That she did not meditate suicide was evident from her having possessed herself of money; yet, unused to the world, young, lovely and inexperienced, what could be her plan? What might not have been her fate?

'Meanwhile I continued for nearly three months confined by the fracture of my limb. Before the lapse of that time, I had begun to crawl about the ground, and now I considered myself as nearly recovered. It had been settled that I should not return to Eton, but be entered at Oxford; and this leap from boyhood to man's estate elated me considerably. Yet still I thought of my poor Ellen, and was angry at her obstinate silence. Once or twice I had, disobeying her command, written to her, mentioning my accident and the kind attentions of Mr Elmore. Still she wrote not; and I began to fear that her illness might have had a fatal termination. She had made me vow so solemnly never to mention her name, never to enquire about her during my absence, that, considering obedience the first duty of a young inexperienced boy to one older than himself, I resisted each suggestion of my affection or my fears, to transgress her orders.

'And now spring came, with its gift of opening buds, odoriferous flowers and sunny genial days. I returned home, and found my family on the eve of their departure for London. My long confinement had weakened me – it was deemed inadvisable for me to encounter the bad air and fatigues of the metropolis, and I remained to rusticate. I rode and hunted, and thought of Ellen, missing the excitement of her conversation, and feeling a vacancy in my heart which she had filled. I began to think of riding across the country from Shropshire to Berkshire for the purpose of seeing her. The whole landscape haunted my imagination – the fields round Eton – the silver Thames – the majestic forest – this lovely scene of Virginia Water – the heath and her desolate cottage – she herself pale, slightly bending from weakness of health, awakening from dark abstraction to bestow on me a kind smile of welcome. It grew into a passionate desire of my heart to behold her, to cheer her as I might by my affectionate attentions, to hear her, and to hang upon her accents of inconsolable despair, as if it had been celestial harmony. As I meditated on these things, a voice seemed for ever to repeat, "Now go, or it will be too late"; while another yet more mournful tone responded, "You can never see her more!"

'I was occupied by these thoughts, as, on a summer moonlit night, I loitered in the shrubbery, unable to quit a scene of entrancing beauty, when I was startled at hearing myself called by Mr Elmore. He came on his way to the coast. He had received a letter from Ireland, which made him think that Miss Eversham was residing near Enniscorthy; a strange place for her to select, but as concealment was evidently her object, not an improbable one. Yet his hopes were not high; on the contrary, he performed this journey more from the resolve to leave nothing undone, than in expectation of a happy result. He asked me if I would accompany him. I was delighted with the offer, and we departed together on the following morning.

'We arrived at Milford Haven, where we were to take our passage. The packet was to sail early in the morning – we walked on the beach, and beguiled the time by talk. I had never mentioned Ellen to Lewis. I felt now strongly inclined to break my vow, and to relate my whole adventure with her, but restrained myself, and we spoke only of the unhappy Clarice – of the despair that must have been hers, of her remorse and unavailing regret.

'We retired to rest, and early in the morning I was called to prepare for going on board. I got ready, and then knocked at Lewis' door. He admitted me, for he was dressed, though a few of his things were still unpacked, and scattered about the room. The morocco case of a miniature was on his table. I took it up. "Did I never show you that?" said Elmore. "Poor dear Clarice! She was very happy when that was painted!"

'I opened it. Rich luxuriant curls clustered on her brow and the snow-white throat; there was a light zephyr appearance in the figure; an expression of unalloyed exuberant happiness in the countenance, but those large dove's eyes, the innocence that dwelt on her mouth, could not be mistaken, and the name of Ellen Burnet burst from my lips.

'There was no doubt: why had I ever doubted? The thing was so plain! Who but the survivor of such a parent, and she the apparent cause of his death, could be so miserable as Ellen? A torrent of explanation followed, and a thousand minute circumstances, forgotten before, now assured us that my sad hermitess was the beloved of Elmore. No more sea voyage – not a second of delay. Our chaise, the horses' heads turned to the east, rolled on with lightning rapidity, yet far too slowly to satisfy our impatience. It was not until we arrived at Worcester that the tide of expectation, flowing all one way, ebbed. Suddenly, even while I was telling Elmore some anecdote to prove that, in spite of all, she would be accessible to consolation, I remembered her ill health and my fears. Lewis saw the change my countenance underwent. For some time I could not command my voice, and when at last I spoke, my gloomy anticipations passed like an electric shock into my friend's soul.

'When we arrived at Oxford, we halted for an hour or two, unable to proceed; yet we did not converse on the subject so near our hearts, nor until we arrived in sight of Windsor did a word pass between us, then Elmore said, "Tomorrow morning, dear Neville, you shall visit Clarice; we must not be too precipitate."

'The morrow came. I arose with that intolerable weight at my breast, which it is grief's worst heritage to feel. A sunny day it was, yet the atmosphere looked black to me; my heart was dead within me. We sat at the breakfast table, but neither ate, and after some restless indecision, we left our inn and (to protract the interval) walked to Bishopsgate. Our conversation belied our feelings: we spoke as if we expected all to be well; we felt that there was no hope. We crossed the heath along the accustomed path. On one side was the luxuriant foliage of the forest; on the other, the widespread moor. Her cottage was situated at one extremity, and could hardly be distinguished, until we should arrive close to it. When we drew near, Lewis bade me go on alone; he would wait my return. I obeyed, and reluctantly approached the confirmation of my fears. At length it stood before me, the lonely cot and desolate garden; the unfastened wicket swung in the breeze; every shutter was closed.

'To stand motionless and gaze on these symbols of my worst forebodings, was all that I could do. My heart seemed to me to call aloud for Ellen – for such was she to me – her other name might be a fiction – but silent as her own life-deserted lips were mine. Lewis grew impatient, and advanced – my stay had occasioned a transient ray of hope to enter his mind – it vanished when he saw me, and her deserted dwelling. Slowly we turned away, and were directing our steps back again, when my name was called by a child. A little girl came running across some fields towards us, whom at last I recognised as having seen before with Ellen. "Mr Neville, there is a letter for you!" cried the child. "A letter? Where? Who?" "The lady left a letter for you. You must go to Old Windsor, to Mr Cooke's; he has got it for you."

'She had left a letter – was she then departed on an earthly journey? "I will go for it immediately. Mr Cooke! Old Windsor! Where shall I find him? Who is he?"

'"Oh, sir, everybody knows him," said the child. "He lives close to the churchyard, he is the sexton. After the burial, Nancy gave him the letter to take care of."

'Had we hoped? had we for a moment indulged the expectation of ever again seeing our miserable friend? Never! O never! Our hearts had told us that the sufferer was at peace – the unhappy orphan with her father in the abode of spirits! Why then were we here? Why had a smile dwelt on our lips, now wreathed into the expression of anguish? Our full hearts demanded one consolation: to weep upon her grave – her sole link now with us, her mourners. There at last my boy's grief found vent in tears, in lamentation. You saw the spot; the grassy mound rests lightly on the bosom of fair Clarice, of my own poor Ellen. Stretched upon this, kissing the scarcely springing turf, for many hours no thought visited me, but the wretched one – that she had lived – and was lost to me for ever!

'If Lewis had ever doubted the identity of my friend with her he loved, the letter put into our hands undeceived him. The handwriting was Miss Eversham's, it was directed to me, and contained words like these:

'*11th April*

'*I have vowed never to mention certain beloved names, never to communicate with beings who cherished me once, to whom my deepest gratitude is due; and, as well as poor bankrupt can, is paid. Perhaps it is a mere prevarication to write to you, dear Horace, concerning them; but – Heaven pardon me! – my disrobed spirit would not repose, I fear, if I did not thus imperfectly bid them a last farewell.*

'*You know him, Neville; and know that he for ever laments her whom he has lost. Describe your poor Ellen to him, and he will speedily see that* she *died on the waves of the murderous Atlantic. Ellen had nothing in common with* her, *save love for, and interest in him. Tell him, it had been well*

96

for him, perhaps, to have united himself to the child of prosperity, the nursling of deep love; but it had been destruction, even could he have meditated such an act, to wed the parrici—.

'I will not write that word. Sickness and near death have taken the sting from my despair. The agony of woe which you witnessed, is melted into tender affliction and pious hope. I am not miserable now. Now! When you read these words, the hand that writes, the eye that sees, will be a little dust, becoming one with the earth around it. You, perhaps he, will visit my quiet retreat, bestow a few tears on my fate, but let them be secret; they may make green my grave, but do not let a misplaced feeling adorn it with any other tribute. It is my last request: let no stone, no name, mark that spot.

'Farewell, dear Horace! Farewell, to one other whom I may not name. May the God to whom I am about to resign my spirit in confidence and hope, bless your earthly career! Blindly, perhaps, you will regret me for your own sakes; but for mine, you will be grateful to the Providence which has snapped the heavy chain binding me to unutterable sorrow, and which permits me from my lowly grass-grown tomb to say to you, I am at peace.

'– ELLEN'

BIOGRAPHICAL NOTE

Mary Shelley was born in London in 1797, the only daughter of the radical writers William Godwin and Mary Wollstonecraft. Her mother died just a few days after her birth and Mary was brought up by her father. In 1814, at the age of seventeen, Mary left England with the writer Percy Bysshe Shelley, whom she married two years later, after his first wife committed suicide. She spent the summer of 1816 at Lake Geneva with Shelley, Lord Byron and John Polidori, and it was here that she began *Frankenstein, or the Modern Prometheus*, the novel for which she is best remembered.

Frankenstein, published in 1818, was followed by *Valperga* (1823) and the futuristic novel, *The Last Man* (1826). In addition, Shelley wrote several biographies and numerous short stories: many with supernatural and science fiction themes. Her novella, *Matilda*, with its controversial subject of an incestuous father–daughter relationship, remained unpublished until 1959.

In 1818 and 1819, two of the Shelleys' young children, Clara and William ('Willhouse'), died while the family was living in Italy. After her husband was drowned in August 1822, Mary Shelley left Italy and moved back to England with their surviving son Percy. Although widowed at the young age of twenty-five, she never remarried. She remained in England, editing her husband's poems, essays and letters, and in later life renounced many of the radical views she had held as a young woman. Mary Shelley died in February 1851.

HESPERUS PRESS CLASSICS

Hesperus Press, as suggested by the Latin motto, is committed to bringing near what is far – far both in space and time. Works written by the greatest authors, and unjustly neglected or simply little known in the English-speaking world, are made accessible through new translations and a completely fresh editorial approach. Through these classic works, the reader is introduced to the greatest writers from all times and all cultures.

For more information on Hesperus Press, please visit our website: **www.hesperuspress.com**

ET REMOTISSIMA PROPE

SELECTED TITLES FROM HESPERUS PRESS